BLUE

ML NYSTROM

———— HOT TREE PUBLISHING ————

LIST OF BOOKS

DRAGON RUNNERS MC
MUTE
STUD
BLUE
TABLE

For information, contact the publisher, Hot Tree Publishing.

WWW.HOTTREEPUBLISHING.COM

EDITING: Hot Tree Editing

COVER DESIGNER: Claire Smith

FORMATTING: RMgraphX

ISBN: 978-1-925853-11-7

This book is dedicated to the Merit Pit Bull Foundation, the doggie foster parents who support it and work with the animals, and all those big-hearted people who adopt rescue animals of any kind.

CHAPTER 1

I woke up to the whines and snuffles of my fifty-pound terrier mix lying beside me. I stifled a groan and lifted my head to see the glowing blue numbers on my old digital clock. 5:02. Time to get up and start another work day. Alarms never had to be set, as the dogs' bladders would go off about the same time every morning.

Toto whined and pawed at the bedclothes again, filling my face with her morning doggie breath. If that didn't get a person up, nothing would.

"I'm up, I'm up," I garbled at the dog, my voice grainy from sleep. I sat up and yawned hugely, mouth wide and teeth showing. I didn't really care. Only the dogs were here to see me and they didn't judge. Four other dogs of various sizes and breed mixes were sprawled on the bed with me. They had their own beds but preferred mine. I had a California king-sized mattress and yet on a nightly basis, I got about a twelve-inch wide strip to balance on at the edge. I pulled back the covers and pulled myself out, dislodging the rest of the canines. Maxx, Dion, Zeke, and Buddy were all rescued shelter dogs and were currently fostering in my care, waiting to find permanent homes. Toto was the only one I had officially adopted and had been with me since puppyhood.

I staggered down the narrow steps to the kitchen door and let the dogs out into the spacious courtyard area. They sniffed around the designated potty place while I stood and watched them for a minute. It was still dark but dawn was creeping over the mountains and lighting up the small downtown area of Bryson City.

The dogs had finished up in the corner of the courtyard and were now settling in for the day. Dion and Zeke were tugging a chew rope between them, Toto was napping in a corner, Buddy was watching a squirrel on the fence with his one good eye, and Maxx was digging a new hole, throwing red dirt on his black fur. I snapped my fingers at him and made a sharp tutting sound. He immediately stopped with one paw still in the soft ground, his head up as he looked at me. His expression warred between *Oops, I got caught* and *Who, me?* I laughed. I was going to miss this little guy. Today was a big day as Maxx had found a forever home and would be taken by his new owners later that afternoon.

Since the dogs were occupied and settled for the time being, I turned toward more pressing business. I make soap. I make a lot of soap and sell it through my little craft store here in this little town in North Carolina. I also stock and sell items like knitted and sewn wares, woodcraft, beadwork, and a bit of pottery from other local artisans. A few years ago, I added a Facebook page to my store and my sales went through the roof. I can barely keep up with my soap production most weeks, and during the height of the summer nearly all my time is spent either at the store or making soap. Tourism is a big pull in this little mountain town with the train rides on the Great Smoky Mountain Railway, the rafting companies working the Nantahala River, the many hiking trails, fishing spots, and campgrounds. The people who come through are voracious for homemade mountain art, and my store turns a nice profit for me and for my suppliers. I do have to say the biggest pull to my store is my soap. It started off as a hobby and grew into this business. I'm forever lucky to have that skill.

I'm a girly girl and like all girly-girl things like lingerie, pretty scented soaps, makeup, hair curlers, and stuff like that. I was still wearing the short silk nightie I slept in and went upstairs to quickly shower and get my day truly started. It was going to be a full one as I had a small mountain of boxes to ship and at least eighty pounds of new product to make. I did take a few minutes to stand in the window to watch the rising sun bathe the street in gold. This was my second-favorite time of the day, when the town was still sleeping and the streets were quiet. A window across from mine lit up, and I ducked behind the white lacy curtain to hide. Deputy Blue was up and starting his day as well. He had just moved into the upper-level apartment in the building across from mine, having called it quits with his on-again, off-again wife. The women who frequented my store were generous with the town gossip. The handsome deputy was a favorite topic, and I got regular updates whenever they came in. I'd heard the divorce had become final after the last round of drama. I could see his short sandy hair tousled from sleep as he ran his hand over his face and head. He stood, stretching his heavy arms high, head hanging back, wearing nothing but a pair of dark boxers. I wasn't close enough to see him fully, but I knew he was built solid and stocky, muscular without the lined definition of a gym rat. He worked out regularly at the gym, but he didn't have the look of a bodybuilder. He was just a man in great shape but probably wouldn't be thrilled to find out his neighbor hid behind a curtain every morning ogling him. It was one part of our morning routine and one he had no clue he participated in.

I watched as he wandered off somewhere in his apartment, probably the bathroom. I headed to my own to shower and get myself ready for a long day. I put on my version of a workday uniform, a light cotton peasant skirt with an ethnic print and a solid ribbed tank top, and went down to my workshop/kitchen area. The smells of the essential oils and fragrances hit my nose and I inhaled deeply of the floral and citrus scents. I made a wide variety of soaps in different colors and designs using a hot process method as well as a cold process. My shop shelves were well organized to keep track of everything. I had already made a list of cold process soaps I needed to make to replenish the ones I was shipping out later. I put on my goggles and gloves to measure and mix up the needed amount of lye solutions in plastic pitchers. They smoked and steamed with the heated chemical reaction. I prided myself on making everything from scratch, but it was a long method and I had to allow time for the solutions to cool. While this was happening, I had time to get my recent orders I'd packed yesterday to the shipping place as soon as it opened at seven. After that was getting coffee, another treat to my daily routine.

The dogs were begging to come with me, but I had no room in my truck bed for them, having to load fourteen large boxes to ship to various stores that bought my soap wholesale. They usually stayed in the courtyard, but sometimes one or two of them hung out with me in the store. Toto mostly, as she was my customer greeter. Everyone in town who came to my store knew her name.

There was a fifteenth box holding several dozen shipping envelopes that I used to send stuff to individual buyers. I was sweating hard by the time I got everything loaded and ready to take to the shipping place. We were at that time of the year when fall cooled the air at night but summer was still trying to hang on during the day.

The shipping place wasn't open yet, but Mountain Perks, my favorite local coffee shop, was. I slipped in to grab a much-needed latte. Pam, the owner, was up and behind the old-fashioned counter working the espresso machine. A few other people were there, more than likely early morning workers for the railroad. I waved to her as the machine hissed and spat out a stream of fragrant goodness. She winked and pulled another cup from the stack. I didn't have to tell her my order as she already knew, a hazelnut latte with a shot of espresso and skim milk.

I turned from the counter to check out her newest displays of mugs and teapots then glanced at my watch. It was six forty-five. The bell over the door rang and Deputy Blue walked in. Right on time. He spotted me, those deep brown eyes of his taking me in, and he nodded a short greeting. My stomach fluttered. I smiled and blinked a greeting back. This was the other part of our morning routine. Sometimes he made it to the coffee shop before I did and sometimes after, but we were there together at some point every morning. He greeted Pam in his low, gruff voice. He didn't have to state his order either. Large Americano. No cream or sugar. Simple and straightforward.

He fiddled with the tourist brochures on display as his cup was being poured. Pam called out for me.

"Morning, Psalm. You're all set." She handed me a steaming paper cup in a cardboard holder. I swiped my card and left a cash tip. As I exited the coffee shop, I glanced in Blue's direction and lifted my cup in a see-you-tomorrow gesture. He nodded again, his face unsmiling. That was it. That was our complete routine and one I'd come to look forward to on a daily basis. Yes, I may have had a small crush on Jason "Blue" Davis that started way back in high school, but I knew I'd probably never act on it.

I'd been married once before. My husband and I had lived in the city of High Point, just a few hours east of here. He'd worked for a furniture company and I managed a local craft store. We met in college where he was studying computer science and I was studying art and business marketing. I fell in love with the tall, lanky, bespectacled man and married him shortly after graduation. We were DINKs in a nice neighborhood in a big modern house with our terrier mix rescue puppy. We were happy and content with our lives, not rich and not going to be rich, just happy.

We had celebrated our six-year anniversary and were talking about having children when Adam became sick. It started out as stomach cramps and we didn't think it was much more than job stress, but it got worse quickly. A few weeks later, we discovered that he had advanced stage four pancreatic cancer. He died less than a month later.

I was devastated. It was like the world shattered around me. Our simple plans for the future had been kids, making secure financial investments, and doing a bit of traveling before settling in a retirement community. It took less than a month for that dream to disappear completely. I can look back now and be grateful that Adam did not linger with months or years of pain and suffering.

Adam was a left-brain thinker, always the logical one. We had money in the bank, a stable investment portfolio, and several life insurance policies thanks to his OCD about planning. Our savings covered the medical bills his insurance didn't, and I was left with a good-sized pile of money. I was also left alone with a big house I didn't need, full of painful memories and broken dreams. I was twenty-eight at that time and by age twenty-nine, I found myself selling the house and moving back to my hometown of Bryson City. My parents still lived outside of the small town and still farmed a bit. I had money to buy my store and home, make the renovations I wanted, open the business, and still have plenty in the bank. Now five years after Adam's death, I'm good. I'm content. I guess I'm happy or at least happy enough.

I'd been on a few dates since my husband died, but no one I'd want to start anything serious with. The one time I tried to sleep with someone else… well, let's just say it didn't go well. He was a nice man and I liked him, but there was no real spark between us. The sex was mechanical at best and even though he got off, he really didn't seem to enjoy it much. I went through the motions, but that was all. We parted ways amicably and since he lived one county over, we didn't see each other as often as we would if we lived in the same town. This helped with any awkwardness that may have cropped up. As it stands, I have my house and store, my rescue foster dogs, friends, colleagues, and parents. Even though it wasn't going to go anywhere, I also had a wonderful daily view of a beautiful man. What else did I really need?

CHAPTER 2

I arrived back to the store about an hour later and went back to my open workroom. The lye solutions were almost cool enough to start mixing. I donned my goggles and gloves again, and started work. I measured the oils and butters I use in the different recipes into several giant five-gallon stock pots and started them heating. My biggest soap molds held ten pounds of soap each. I could make bigger molds, but then the weight and size of the soap loafs would be hard for me to handle. I'm a very petite woman and even though I'm not particularly weak, I'm also not very muscular. When I was working, I kept my blonde hair tied up in a ponytail and under a bandana to hang down my back, as the long, thick strands had a tendency to get in the way. Lye burns were nothing to sneeze at, so I always wore protection when handling the solutions and the raw soap. I'd like to keep my blue eyes and as it would only take one splash to blind me, my goggles were covered with a full-face shield.

In between mixing, I had to open the store. No one was

on the street yet, but there would be a lot of foot traffic later in the morning. I added the essential oils to the batch I was mixing and kept an eye on the front door. Lavender, bergamot, and clary sage went into this one as well as a swirl of lavender, white, and teal colorings. The next would be lemongrass and avocado in a solid pale green. I would add finely ground, dried lemongrass to that one.

A few people wandered in and poked around, watching me work. Holly came in, the woman who made the doll clothes and helped run the store a few days a week. I waved a soap-covered glove at her. Some of my other artists came in to work the store occasionally and meet the people who bought their wares, but Holly was one of my regulars and a big help.

The morning blurred into the afternoon. Holly left, and I was working the store as well as slicing a soap loaf into bars. This one was scented in Japanese Cherry Blossom and I had used white, forest green, and dark burgundy as the colors. A fairly steady stream of people had come through and I'd received a number of internet orders that I'd already packed up and had ready for the shipping run the next morning. The dogs were out in the courtyard except for Toto. She was lounging on her bed near the door. Being the most senior of the dogs meant she could stay inside and greet customers. She'd had a stroke a few months back and I was having to give her shots and daily pills for her arthritis, but I wasn't ready to give her the big shot just yet. She was the last tie I had to Adam. Maybe this was a selfish act, but so far she wasn't in pain or suffering. Our vet, Dr. Lindsey Jackson, had told me at our last visit that I wasn't wrong either way at this point, so I chose to keep her here just a bit longer. I was sure she would have advised me differently if it was truly time.

Being a Tuesday, I closed the store at six, changed into frayed jeans and a T-shirt, and left to take the dogs to the dog park where they could run and play without the confines of the courtyard. Maxx's new family would be meeting us there and I'd have one less dog to feed later.

Walking four dogs took some stamina. Toto didn't go, as she just couldn't make it that far and keeping up with the younger dogs wasn't easy for her. I ran and played with the dogs as well, tossing several balls and toys for them to catch and bring back. I had poop bags in one pocket for accidents and treats in the other. Zeke ran up with a slobber-covered tennis ball, which I took from his mouth and threw. He barked and took off after it. Buddy slumped down, panting contentedly at my feet, and rolled for a belly rub. Maxx and Dion were playing tug of war with a rope toy. Other dogs were around with their owners and I had to keep a sharp eye on all four of mine.

There was a playground for children on the other side of the parking lot. I saw Blue drive up in his deputy car and my heart jumped a little. He and his two kids climbed out with backpacks and headed to the equipment. It looked like he'd picked them up from school that day. Now my focus was split between the kids playing on the monkey bars, my dogs running around, and Blue leaning on a swing set. His arms were folded and he was watching his kids and never looked in my direction. I barely noticed when a family of Mom, Dad, and two preteen girls approached me.

"Ms. Kopolove?" I turned to the female voice and smiled. The goal was to get my fosters adopted to forever homes, but there was still that bittersweet tingle when one of them moved out.

"Hi, Angie," I greeted and held out my hand. "He's right over there. Do you have a leash and treats?"

Angie smiled back. "Yes, we have them right here. We bought a dog bed today, food, dishes, the whole nine yards. The girls are so excited!"

I nodded and turned to call Maxx to me. He let go of the toy, looked up with his ears forward in his *Who me?* look, and ignored me completely. He bounded over to the two kids who were sitting on the ground, patting their legs and calling, "Here, Maxx, here, Maxxie!" He climbed all over the laughing girls to lick at their faces. They played with the jumping dog for a few minutes before snapping on a leash. I hugged and petted him before they led him away. Tears pricked at my eyes when he paused and turned back. I knew he was confused, but the girls fawned over him as they lifted him to the strange car, petting and talking to him. He would be fine, spoiled rotten more than likely.

I heard some shouting and my attention was drawn back to the kids' park. Jonelle, Blue's ex-wife, was there now, picking up the kids. She was yelling something and gesturing wildly. I couldn't hear her words, but it was obvious she wasn't happy. The kids were cringing, their heads bowed. Blue was talking, not yelling, but his arms were stiff at his sides and his fists were balled up tight. I didn't think he was the type to ever hit a woman, but Jonelle would be trying for anyone. She and I were the same age and I remembered her from back in school as being unpredictable. She could be either sticky sweet or she could go off frequently on someone when she didn't get her way or was displeased. That hadn't changed in the years since we were kids. It was also no secret she'd been involved in some serious drug use and even had to go into rehab for a while. Blue was a few years ahead of me in school and I remembered him being on the football and wrestling teams. How he and Jonelle fell in love enough to marry and have kids was a mystery. I gasped as Jonelle swung her hand to crack across Blue's face. He caught her arm before she made contact and said something to her. She screamed at him and I heard "fucking bastard!" from across the lot. The kids quietly picked up their backpacks and climbed into Jonelle's black Camaro. Her tires screeched as she pulled out of the parking lot, almost daring Blue to do something about it. He stood there for a moment, statue still, then got in his squad car and drove off himself.

I sighed. My heart went out to those two kids. I could only imagine what they were going through. My parents were still together and I'd never seen them even argue. Pick at each other, yes, but never had they been into a knock-down, drag-out fight. My sadness for the kids was tempered with anger at their mom and dad. Jonelle's temper was legendary around town and I couldn't for the life of me understand how Blue could allow his two children to get in a car with her and drive away. I didn't know exactly what their lives were like, and I did try to understand more than criticize, but for the life of me I couldn't wrap my head around Blue's spineless approach to his kids' care. It made me want to slap him myself.

I called my remaining dogs to me. Later they would look for Maxx, but in the doggie world, their grief would be short, as they still had each other.

Back at my house, I closed up the courtyard and fed everyone, including myself. Grilled cheese and soup from a can weren't a culinary experience, but cooking for one was a pain because by that time at night, I was ready to relax. The nights were becoming dark earlier. I thought about taking a bubble bath but decided on TV and a glass of wine. I was surfing the channels looking for something to catch my interest when a light across the street came on. I moved over and saw Blue in his window. He opened the little fridge in his apartment and pulled out a bottle of beer. I felt guilty for spying on him, but it was hard to look away. He walked around a bit, then put the beer back in the fridge unopened. I knew what that meant. He turned off the light and left the apartment. A moment later, I heard and saw him pull out of the narrow alley next to the building on his motorcycle. He drove off with a roar. He would return later, early morning sometime, somehow managing to still meet me at the coffee shop on time for our secret routine. I didn't know where he went or what he did. I just knew this was a frequent thing. As angry at him as I was an hour ago, I still hurt for him.

I stood up myself and put on my favorite yoga pants

and big sweatshirt. I went down to my workroom, as sleep would be impossible until I heard the returning growl of the big navy blue Harley. Blue had no knowledge of the vigil I kept for him during nights like these, but I'd had problems with insomnia during my marriage as well. I looked over my shelves of oils, butters, waxes, and the other bits of my trade, seeking inspiration. Hmm…. How 'bout a new flavor of lip balm? Chocolate mint? Cherry lime? One recipe made close to two hundred tubes and would take a few hours to finish.

I took out my big bowls, digital scale, empty tubes, and filling trays, and got to work.

***

Blue sat on his bike and looked over the sleeping North Carolina town from the bluff. He lifted the cigarette to his lips and took a long puff, wishing it was something other than tobacco. The smoke curled in the cool night air over his head to mingle with his breath. Being an inactive member of the Dragon Runners MC, the son of its president and queen, and a sheriff's deputy didn't mean he was immune to the occasional illegal behavior, but he couldn't take any chances on anything that would jeopardize his job. Jonelle had come to the park earlier to pick up the kids and had been in rare form. Demanding more money, claiming she needed it for new school clothes for the kids and he had to pony it up right then and there. He dared to ask about the extra he gave her last month for new school clothes and she had flown into one of her hissing rages. She tried to hit him, but he'd already been the recipient of those claws before. Three faint parallel scars across his cheek proved it. He would never hit a woman, not even when that woman took a swing at him, but he'd be damned if he allowed her to ever mark him again, especially in front of the kids.

He wanted to sue for full custody, but he had no real home to take them to right now. Nearly all his money went to alimony and child support. The craptastic apartment he could afford on what was left was little more than a couple of small, bare rooms. The only redeeming quality was he had a nice view of the old Bowers house with its white siding and grayish-blue trim. He could move back to the Lair with his parents, but what did that say when a thirty-six-year-old man had to move back home? The Lair was a giant lodge on the Dragon Runners compound that housed rooms for the club as well as the home of Betsey and Brick Davis, his parents and the leaders of the club. He didn't think the town council would appreciate it either.

From the observation point on the bluffs, he had a pretty good downward view overlooking Main Street, and noticed a faint light on in the lower half of the Bowers house across the street from his apartment. He made an educated guess that Psalm was up again, working in her store. He'd noticed the lights coming on during past nights when he was restless and roaming. If he was on the street, at just the right angle, he could sometimes spot her bustling around her work area. She was on the short side, not much over five-foot-tall maybe, and petite all over. She had straight blonde hair that always seemed to shine and flow like liquid gold across her shoulders. Sometimes she wore it in a clip while she worked, but his favorite way to see it was when she let it hang free and loose. She was always made up, but not overblown like many of the women he knew at the clubhouse. Jonelle had a shit ton of makeup and wore it constantly as well, but somehow the two looks were different.

Blue drew in another lungful of smoke and let it out slowly. How had life gotten this way? He'd thought by this age he should have been well into his career, his kids doing well, with a content wife, secure future, halfway through the mortgage payments, and well on his way to a long and happy life. Instead he was struggling to stay afloat, worried constantly about his kids, and dealing with an ex-wife who was more like a banshee than a woman. He didn't even remember why he married her in the first place. If there was any love between them once upon a time, it was long dead and buried.

He finished his cigarette and pinched the end before putting it in his jacket pocket. There were strict rules about littering on the bluffs and the odd cigarette had been known to start forest fires. As a man of the law, Blue felt he had to follow the same rules he enforced, although there were a few he bent from time to time. He mounted up to go back down the worn trail to the town he was sworn to protect. Maybe now he could sleep a few hours. He had to be up later and would see Psalm at the coffee shop at her usual time. Hazelnut latte with a shot of espresso and skim milk. She would probably be shocked at how much he looked forward to their daily nod and blink.

CHAPTER 3

The morning started as usual. The dogs woke me up a little after five and I blearily let them out to take care of business. The property used to have a number of outbuildings, but those and most of the land surrounding the house was sold after the good doctor who previously owned the house passed. I called it the courtyard as there was a gazebo in the middle, a few trees, and several marked flower bed areas that were surrounded with stone pathways. I always thought the previous owner had visions of garden parties and such when he used the place as a bed-and-breakfast. My dogs pretty much made gardening impossible and they used the enclosed gazebo as a community dog house. An eight-foot-high wood privacy fence kept my dogs in and onlookers out.

I went through my routine and saw that Blue was up too. He really should have curtains. My mouth went dry at the sight of him in only a towel, wet from a recent shower. He turned and dropped it on the bed, giving me a great view of his perfect tight ass. *Oh yeah!* I watched as he stretched his arms over his head. It was too far away to see his back muscles flex, but I imagined what they would look like up close, flawless as a marble sculpture. Michelangelo would be jealous. He turned around and I got an eyeful before I realized he was facing the window. I ducked down, thinking that the curtains probably hid me enough that he hadn't seen me ogling him. Even so, I hunched over, awkwardly moving across my room to grab my own shower and start my day.

I was running a bit behind when I drove my pile of boxes to the shipping place. I needed the coffee but wanted to make sure this bunch made the morning route. I piled them high on the hand truck I kept in the back of my pickup and heaved the thing over to push it into the store. The load was top-heavy and started to topple. I grabbed for it and almost lost the whole pile, but a khaki-clad arm stopped the tower of boxes from tipping and settled them back on the hand truck. I looked up into the deep brown eyes of the man whose naked ass I had admired just an hour or so ago. My heart sped up a bit as butterflies blossomed in my stomach, and I hoped my face wasn't turning red.

"Um… thanks, Deputy Davis," I said, proud of the way I maintained a steady voice.

"No problem, Ms. Kopolove," he replied, just as steadily. He wheeled the hand truck around and tilted it back further to hold the boxes in place. "Get the door and I'll get these inside."

I noticed he didn't ask, he ordered, but I wasn't going to point that out. I opened the door and he pushed the heavy contraption easily over the threshold bump where I usually had to wrestle it.

"This all you got?" he asked, setting the hand truck upright and lifting the first box onto the counter. The shipping clerk brought out his scanner and zapped the barcodes on the labels I'd already prepared.

"Yes, that's all for this load," I answered.

He nodded and continued to place box after box on the counter. "You getting coffee after you're finished here?" He leaned on the hand truck handle and wiped a hand over his moist brow.

"That's the plan." I laughed lightly. The butterflies were back.

The clerk finished up and I signed the paper and swiped my credit card. Blue waited and walked silently with me the short distance to the coffee shop. Pam saw us coming and smiled big. She had both our coffees ready by the time we came in, Blue holding the door open for me. I had to brush close enough to him to enter that I could smell his masculine aroma. He didn't wear any aftershave and only smelled like clean male, but his scent still tickled my nose. Those butterflies were soaring through my middle again. Before I could swipe my card, he paid for both coffees and handed me mine.

"Thank you, Deputy. You didn't have to do that, you know." I muttered, taking the first sip and groaning. Pam was a coffee artist!

"No problem, Ms. Kopolove," he said again, his voice low and gruff. "You ship that many boxes every day?"

I nodded. "I have a load every morning. Sometimes a

few less and sometimes a few more."

"Business must be pretty good."

"Umm… yes. Everyone needs soap, and my vendors are constantly asking for more. I like pretty things and try to make all my soaps pretty. People seem to like it and my vendors have said they sell out frequently."

"Nice problem to have." He smiled. "Plenty of people would love to be in your shoes."

"Yes, I'm sure they would."

I looked him in the eye for a moment and then had to look away. I wasn't sure what else to say or do as we stood there awkwardly sipping our coffees. I could feel myself blushing as my brain scrambled for something to say.

"I'd better get back to the store," I finally said. "Thanks again for the coffee. Maybe my treat tomorrow?"

"We'll see." That was usually manspeak for "not a chance," but maybe I could do something nice for him. He did help me get my stuff to the shipping place without disaster.

"Um—thank you for helping me. Come by the shop and I'll give you a soap of your choice," I said as we walked out the door. Again, he held it open for me. Some women didn't like men doing this, but I really enjoyed being treated like a lady and appreciated those gentlemanly gestures.

"Might do that," he uttered and lifted the hand truck into the back of my pickup. I was pretty sure this was still manspeak for "I doubt it." "I'll see you at the shipping place tomorrow morning, Ms. Kopolove." He nodded and moved to his own vehicle. "You need help lifting them boxes at the store, just let me know."

I was on cloud nine. Yes, I still had that high school crush and hoped Blue would come in to see my shop, but reality was he had no reason to do so. Back in high school, I was the pretty, popular, good girl, a cheerleader, and a class officer. I made the honor roll and stuff like that. I even won the title of Homecoming Queen my junior year and got to ride in the Thanksgiving Day parade in a fluffy pink dress. I still have the sparkly rhinestone crown. Blue and I never talked much in school. We weren't really friends, but we, being involved in athletics, were somewhat in the same circle. He was a bit of a wild child and an up-and-coming member of the local motorcycle club of which his parents were the leaders. I guess you could say we knew of each other but didn't know each other. He didn't know I carried a torch for him then and he doesn't know it now either.

The day progressed like every other day. Greet customers, fill online orders as they came in, take pictures of new stock and post on the website, and, of course, make soap. I was cooking a liquid castille soap base made from pure olive oil to fill an order for a store in Asheville, and the phone rang while I was mixing in eucalyptus essential oil to the hot liquid batter.

It was Dr. Jackson. She was part of an animal rescue and knew all my dogs. I already knew what was coming.

"Hey, Psalm, how are you?" she opened politely. "Store doing well?"

"I'm good. The store is good. What do you have for me?" I asked, laughing a bit.

She laughed as well. "You already know I have a placement, don't you? Well, this one's kinda special. Do you remember that multi-state dog fighting ring that was busted up a while back?"

"Yes, I do," I replied, holding the phone with my chin against my shoulder so I could free up my hands. I needed to get one of those Bluetooth thingies really soon. "It was one of the biggest ever found."

"Yup. Well you know there was a bunch of dogs there that were treated and rehabbed. A few had to be put down, but the rest are being fostered out now. I got a call about one yesterday. He's all healed up but needs a good foster place. You think you're up for that?"

"Pit bull, I'm assuming?" I asked while stirring the soapy solution. The pungent scent of the eucalyptus wafted from the giant pot, and the steam made my face damp and shiny. My hair was up in a messy bun at the top of my head and starting to fall apart in the wet heat.

"Um, yes… and, um…." Dr. Jackson's voice was different. My ears pricked up.

"Something wrong with him?" I asked, putting the extra-long spoon down and wiping at my face, probably smearing what was left of my makeup.

"His name is Sam and he was one of the big gladiators. He did a lot of the really fierce fighting and has a lot of scars to prove it. When the raid happened, he was in the pit, but this time on the losing end. He was pretty torn up and probably would have died there if the rescuers hadn't found him in time. Nasty business. I can't understand why anyone would condone or promote this kind of cruelty! Makes me sick."

I agreed with her. I hoped the people responsible stayed in jail for a good long time.

"I do have an opening, but will he be okay with my other dogs?" I had worked with pitties before, including a few fighting dogs, but those were at the shelter. I've never had one to foster long-term.

"He's good with the other dogs at the shelter, but—well, you'd need to see him. I'll be blunt, Psalm. This dog has been through hell and back. He's super big, he's super strong, he's super smart, and he's super scared. We expected more aggression, but he spends his time cowering and hiding. Barely comes out of his crate. Food is an issue. He eats as if he thinks it will be taken away from him and we're pretty sure he was starved, but he doesn't show enough of a food aggression to the workers or to other dogs to be concerning. He needs a kind, patient hand and I think yours is one of the best. Can you take him, or do you want to meet him first?"

My heart bled just a little for the abused animal, but part of being a good pet owner and good foster mom was being responsible.

"Yes, I'd like to meet him first, but here at home with the other dogs. I'd like to see how he reacts to them before committing. Can we make that happen?"

"I've got him here at the clinic's kennels. Have a plan in mind?" Dr. Jackson asked. I could hear her rustling some papers in the background.

"How 'bout you bring him around tomorrow night?

If you'll take the other dogs to the park for their nightly run, I can spend a little time with Sam. Toto will stay here as well. She doesn't do the park much anymore and she's a good influence to have around," I answered, trying to think ahead. "Sam can get a sense of the place, I can get a sense of him, and when you bring the dogs back home, they can meet each other on home turf. There's a street festival this weekend and if he stays, I'd like to get him settled in before the crowds come through."

"That would be perfect! Great! I really appreciate this," the vet said. She was one of my favorite people.

We chatted for a few more minutes and then hung up. I was pouring the batch of liquid soap into bottles when I heard the store bell ring. I didn't jump every time someone came in, letting whoever it was browse for a bit, but I did greet everyone.

"Hi! Welcome to Soap-n-stuff. Please let me know if you have any questions," I called out while watching the level of a filling bottle.

"Take your time," I heard a very familiar masculine voice say.

I almost overfilled the bottle. I hurriedly capped it off and turned to look through the workroom window facing the front counter. Blue was in my store, bending down to pet Toto who was napping in the sun from the window. Her tail thumped on the floor in a doggie greeting, but she didn't bother to get up.

Blue is in my store! And I was dripping with sweat, my hair was frazzled, and my makeup was gone. If I could have disappeared into the floor, I would have dug the hole in record time.

Blue was in his brown and khaki uniform. He looked both official and officially hot. I felt those butterflies start again, and when he looked up at me from his position on the floor, they flew south. It had been such a long time that I'd crushed on this man and I didn't know why it was still happening. I'd been married and loved another man, for Pete's sake! I guess old habits die hard.

I shook it off and put on my best, most relaxed, easy smile. My appearance bothered me but it couldn't be helped.

"Hello, Deputy. Decided on that soap I promised? I have a number of male scents you may like."

"Not here for soap, Ms. Kopolove. Just checking on street permits for the festival." He grunted, standing up and walking to the front counter. "New thing the council started to increase revenues. Too many town vendors setting up side tables without paying space fees like other outside sellers."

I frowned. The town council was constantly claiming a lack of funding and was always trying to come up with more and more ideas to make more money. Some of them were legit but others pushed the bounds of the law. Either way, it meant I had to sell more soap to keep up.

"Doesn't seem right for me to pay a fee to set up a table outside my own store and on my own private property, Deputy," I said crossly. "I already pay some pretty high taxes that should cover my obligation to the town. If I don't pay the street fee, does that mean I can't open?"

"You can still open for the festival, but it does mean

someone else can reserve and take the sidewalk spot in front." He fingered a bar of Mayan Gold soap colored in swirls of deep yellow, black, and white. He brought the bar to his nose and inhaled the masculine, spicy scent deeply. It was one of my best sellers and I could imagine this scent doing well for him.

"That's ridiculous," I stated, and I meant it. I crossed my arms over my chest and huffed a stray piece of hair from my face, my appearance forgotten in my anger. "We just had another property tax increase that was supposed to help fund pay raises for your department. From what I understand, that hasn't happened. Now they're asking for more?"

"I agree with you, but I can't do anything about it. I'm still waiting on that raise myself. You can bring it up at the next town council meeting, but for now you'll need to pay the table fee or give up the spot. For what it's worth, I am sorry you're having to pay extra and you're not alone. Nearly everyone I've talked to today doesn't like this new rule too much." He put the soap down and picked up another one. Coconut and lime scented on a diagonal of white and teal with a yellow stripe in between. He smelled that one too.

I huffed again. "Thank you for telling me." I tried to keep my miffed attitude, but I've always been slow to anger. I was probably the one person in the world who didn't get mad when someone with a cartful of groceries got in line at the ten items or less express lane at the grocery store. I sighed and let it go, my arms dropping by my side. This really wasn't Blue's fault. He really was only doing his job, and it wasn't an easy one. I was sure more than one store owner had already raked him over the coals for this decision that was out of his control. He looked tired, his face long and the hint of dark circles under his eyes. It wasn't in me to make it worse. "I'm sorry for giving you a hard time. I know you're just doing what you have to do and I really appreciate you for it."

He looked up at me from his perusal of my soaps. I smiled and blinked at him, mirroring my usual morning greeting. On impulse, I plucked a pale purple bar of soap from the display and handed it to him.

"Here, please take this one as a thank-you gift from me to you. I know lavender is not the manliest of scents, but it is calming to the soul and you look like you could use a bit of calm." I pressed the pale purple bar into his hand and he closed his blunt fingers around it. "You probably aren't supposed to take gifts while in uniform, but surely a bar of soap isn't a big deal."

He stared at me for a moment and grunted before dropping his eyes to the bar. He gripped it hard, and I saw his jaw tighten. "Thank you, Psalm," he said roughly, finally using my first name but unable to meet my eyes as he spoke.

He jammed his hat on his head and muttered a "haveanicedayma'am" to me before practically running from the store. Maybe he didn't like lavender?

***

Blue hustled down the sidewalk, intending to finish his rounds of the businesses that were on the vendor list for the street festival as quickly as possible. No one was happy about the new fees associated with the festival and he had even been cussed out by several. Psalm was the only one who didn't blame the messenger. The pretty shop owner had even given him a gift, one he still clutched in his hand. He raised it to his nose and inhaled the scent. She was right. It was calming. Or maybe it was because she was the one who'd made it and handed it to him. Somehow that made the pale lavender bar more special. He tucked it into his shirt pocket so he would be able to smell it for the rest of the day.

CHAPTER 4

I spent the rest of my day experimenting with sample recipes, making more large batches, and working with customers. It was a good day in that the sun had brought out a lot of people to the town. Other vendors would be arriving tomorrow morning to set up for the big festival that would happen Friday and Saturday. I enjoyed the festivals and made a good profit during them. Lots of people were already thinking about Christmas gifts. Maybe it wouldn't be so bad having someone else set up in front of the store. Might increase foot traffic overall. I decided to let it go and let someone else have a chance at making some business happen this weekend.

When I took the dogs to the park that night, I wondered with a little tummy flutter if I would see Blue with his kids again. He wasn't there, but they were with their grandmother, Betsey. She was one of my regulars and the opposite of any grandmother I'd ever known. She was in her customary tight jeans, black-heeled boots, long-sleeved shirt with the shoulders cut out and her "property" vest with the Dragon Runners symbol on the back. She kept her hair long and dyed bright red. Some women had made comments about being someone's "property," saying it was disrespectful and demeaning. Betsey didn't seem to mind, and, honestly, she was about as far from property as you could get. She did what she wanted when she wanted, always spoke her mind, and was not an easily intimidated person. She was also fiercely loyal to the club, her old man Brick, and her grandkids. Betsey was the kind of mama bear you'd want in your corner. All the "old ladies" I knew were just as confident of themselves and their place. Molly Stalone and Tambre Bearclaw were two of the other longtime club women. The three made a powerful trinity of womanhood. Confident, hardworking, secure in their places, and, for the most part, well respected in the town. If that's what it meant to be "property" of a Dragon Runners member, that didn't seem to be so bad.

Betsey spotted me and waved. Her granddaughter, Michelle, was about six, and was currently swinging, pulling her legs and body back and forth to go higher and higher. Cody was a little younger, but I wasn't sure by how many years. He was climbing on a contraption that looked like a half moon. He pulled himself to the top and sat on the uppermost bit, grinning and waving his triumph to Betsey. She clapped her enthusiasm.

All of a sudden, his face changed. His happy smile dropped and he scrambled down the hexagonal bars. Michelle stopped her swinging abruptly with a puff of playground dust and a spray of mulch. She got up from the strap that formed the swing's chair and walked slowly to get her school backpack. I saw Jonelle in the parking lot as she climbed out of her car and leaned on the door. Her arms were crossed and her nose high in the air. She didn't speak to or go near Betsey. She just yelled for the kids to get a move on and get in the car. The two children went from happy, laughing kids to quiet robots in an instant. Betsey waved at them as they climbed into their mother's car and drove away. It didn't take a genius to figure out she was frustrated and couldn't do anything about it.

It was the kids I felt sorry for the most. They were the helpless ones as they were completely under the control of the different adults in their life and those adults couldn't even control themselves. Adam and I had just adopted a puppy and were thinking about kids when we found out about his sickness. I didn't get the chance to be a mother and perhaps never would. It was amazing how life interfered with plans.

My mutts were my kids. I called them to me and went home to finish my evening routine. Or at least I tried to. I ended up tossing and turning, unable to turn my brain off. Thoughts of Blue, his children, and what was going on in his life disturbed me and even though I was not directly involved, I still felt empathy toward the suffering family. I lit a candle I'd scented with vetiver and bergamot to promote calm and ease. It didn't work very well. I finally gave up sleeping with a sigh and went down once again to putter around in the workroom. If I couldn't shut down enough to sleep, I'd at least get something done. Maybe try making some other calming scented candles. Even if they didn't work for me, they might for someone else.

CHAPTER 5

I watched as Lindsey drove up to my store just after closing. She had the dog in her back seat and he'd crammed himself against the floorboards. It took her several tries to get him out, but he was pretty well leash-trained and didn't fight once she snapped the blue leather strap onto his collar. He climbed out of the car and pancaked flat to the pavement, cowering down as low as he could go. My heart went out to the poor confused animal.

His coat was brindled, and he was big, broad, and muscular, the bodybuilder version of a dog. His back and shoulder muscles were tensed up as he gripped the ground, showing off huge roundness and deep delineation. This dog was a true athlete and it showed.

He also showed a tremendous amount of abuse. His muzzle, face, and neck were pockmarked with scars from many past fights. His ears were nothing more than tiny stumps, cut away as fighting dog owners did so that opponents would have less to grab with snapping jaws.

Other scars both long and short covered his body, back, and flanks.

I cringed along with the mixed-up and scared animal. He'd really been through hell in his previous life. I hoped I could help him get to a better place.

Lindsey brought the paperwork for me to sign and gave me an update on Sam. She took the other dogs, except Toto, to the park and left me and Sam to become acquainted. I led him into the courtyard to scent the other dogs and watch his reaction. The hair on his back stayed flat and he didn't show any aggression, but he was very cautious, still crawling and pancaking when in an open area. I knew he'd be more comfortable in a closed-in environment and brought him to the corner bistro table I kept in one corner. This was not my first rodeo with an abused animal and he did what I fully expected him to do. He cowered behind the flimsy piece of furniture, eager to have any sort of protection he could find. I sat next to him on the ground, coming down to his level. My pockets were full of bacon treats and I was ready to simply sit with him until the rest of the pack came home. I talked to him, keeping my voice calm, low, and slow, staying near but leaving him an escape route should he need it. I didn't think I was his last hope, but Lindsey had mentioned she thought I was his best.

I stayed there a long time talking to him. I told him about my other dogs and how they came to me before finding their forever homes. I told him about my life with Adam and my soap craft. I told him about how sorry I was he'd been treated so badly and promised he would find peace here. He didn't move from his spot until Toto appeared. She came through the back doggie door that I had forgotten to secure earlier. I held my breath, not knowing how Sam would react.

Sam sat up and took interest in her approach, but his back hair didn't raise and he didn't growl. Toto was walking stiffly as her arthritis was flaring again. She stopped when she got close to my seated position and finally noticed Sam. Both dogs looked at each other straight in the eye and were still. Toto was the first one to move. She nestled her way between my thighs and pushed the top of her head into my chest. This was her version of a doggie hug and had been her habitual greeting ever since puppyhood. Sam just watched. Toto flumped down with a sigh, curling up in the crook of my legs and putting her head and paw on my thigh. She grunted and sighed as she closed her eyes, as if saying "I'm where I want to be."

It was then that Sam approached, sniffing at the older dog's head and ears. He looked up, his big gold eyes meeting mine for the first time. They were still full of confusion but also intelligence. Best of all, he didn't show any fear of me or Toto. He inhaled in several short bursts, taking in my scent, and seemed to come to his own decision.

With a flump of his own, he curled up next to me and put his head near Toto's. She rewarded him with a lick to his stumpy ear. We stayed that way, me on the ground with the two dogs, stroking both canine heads until the sound of the other dogs came to my ears. The happy barks and yips stirred up Sam and he looked to me for guidance, but it was Toto's calm presence that helped the most. She didn't move other than to raise her head at the noise. Buddy, Zeke, and Dion scrambled into the courtyard and were expecting to be off-leash immediately but stopped short when they saw a new pack member. Since they were used to dogs coming in and out of our pack, this was not a big deal. Buddy came up to greet and sniff, followed by Zeke. Sam stiffened but stayed easy and didn't hunch in an attack position. Toto put her paw over his as if saying "chill out, it's just the kids coming home."

After greetings and smells, Lindsey left to go home to her family with a wave and I got everyone fed and ready for bed. It was later than normal, but I still went through my nighttime routine. I glanced to see if Blue was home yet, but his lights were still off. The dogs piled on the bed with me and Toto climbed up the steps I'd put in for her to use. Sam watched but wasn't sure about joining in. He really was big and I didn't know how he would fit with the others crowded around. Toto woofed lightly at him and he leapt easily, his scarred body full of power. He settled in next to Toto, treating her like a mentor.

Sleeping with that many bodies in my bed was not easy, but I managed. I also managed not to worry about Blue and fell asleep surrounded by warm doggie bodies.

* * *

Blue opened the door to his tiny apartment and lightly tossed his keys on what passed for a kitchen counter. He pulled a beer out of the half-size refrigerator, twisted off the top, and took a long, cold swallow. He briefly thought about riding up to his spot on the bluffs but decided against it. The day had been long but uneventful for a change, so maybe he could actually sleep tonight. He had called his children earlier to check on them and listened to them chatter about their day. Jonelle was either in a good mood or she wanted something, as she didn't try to cut the call short. He took another pull on the beer and went to his window to look across the street. The house was dark, so he assumed Psalm was sleeping. He imagined her bevy of canines were around her.

Thoughts of what she would look like in her bedroom and in her bed filled his head. He imagined her bedroom to be soft and feminine like the woman herself. She probably slept in lacy nighties with pretty ribbons. He felt his body harden as an image appeared in his brain of her in a pale pink nightgown just see-through enough to tease but still be tasteful. He turned away from the window, feeling a just a little creeperish. Looking into someone's windows was a serious invasion of privacy, although he could almost swear he'd spotted her watching him just out of the shower a few mornings ago. If she did see him, she got a show.

If his life circumstances were different, he would probably welcome the attention from the pretty shopkeeper and return it with some of his own. As it stood, he had too much to focus on as it was, and adding in a woman in any capacity wouldn't be right. He stripped off down to his black briefs and climbed into his own bed. The last thing he did before he turned out the light was take the lavender bar of soap sitting on his nightstand and inhale the fragrance deeply.

CHAPTER 6

Hundreds of people crowded Main Street the second night of the fall festival. The street itself was blocked off, and the foot traffic was tremendous. It helped that the weather was warm and clear, although the nights were getting cooler now that fall was setting in. A band stage was set up close to the square and I could see Stud's group was currently playing. He was a great bassist and singer and had frequently used his Viking, blond, good looks to flirt and gain notoriety, living up to his name. All that was in the past now as everyone knew he was off the market. Eva was one of my biggest sellers with her beautiful quilts, and Stud was her old man. Both were members of the Dragon Runners MC and very good friends of mine as well as business partners. Stud was the lawyer and accountant for the club and helped me keep my books on the side.

I sniffed at the air appreciatively, taking in the tang of cooking barbecue mixed with the sugary scent of fried funnel cakes. I was so ready for some food! I'd been on my feet all day with people coming in and out of my store. Quite a number were just lookie-loos, but lots of people were there to buy. One lady nearly cleaned me out of bath bombs. She bought all the purple, pink, blue, and gold ones for office Christmas gifts and asked when I'd be making more. It was probably a record sales day and I would be checking those totals later when I could remember how my knees bent.

"You look plumb tuckered!" I heard a woman say. Molly, one of my regulars and an MC old lady, came in the door. She and Betsey had been working the MC's barbecue booth during the day and apparently had shut down for the night. In her hand was a big white Styrofoam box with that heavenly scent wafting from it. My mouth watered. Nothing was better than Betsey's homemade barbecue. The club had a big community party every year at Halloween and served massive amounts of the succulent meat. I'd gone to the event for years growing up. Now, I went there as a craft vendor.

"We ran out of 'cue a little while ago, but I saved some for ya," she trilled. I liked Molly a lot. Her enthusiastic nature was always present and she never seemed to lose her good mood.

"Thank you so much, Molly!" I said gratefully, taking the heavy container. There must be several pounds in it, enough for four or five meals. "I've been craving some of this all day. How much do I owe you?"

Molly shook her curly head. "You don't owe nothin', girlfriend! As much as you help out the club sisters? You know you're an honorary member, just without an old man to make it official. Might could help with that, if you ever wanna come up to the Lair on a party night. There's plenty of single men lookin' for a good woman."

The Lair was the club's compound and headquarters. It was a huge log cabin lodge sitting on private property at the top of a huge hill that overlooked the river and the recently reopened Rivers Edge Bar. The bar was owned by the MC and the original had burned down at Christmas this past year. Rumors had flown around town that it was arson caused by another club but the Dragon Runners were extremely secretive about it. Eva MacAteer and her family's business, Irish Pub Builders, were hired to bring it back to life and they did a magnificent job. Eva fell in love with Stud and stayed. The rest of her family went somewhere else to continue on their own paths. Eva was one of my artists in that she could design and sew. I couldn't keep her lounge pants in stock; they sold almost as soon as I put them on display. Her lap quilts also were big sellers and some townswomen had commissioned wedding dresses from her.

"I may come up sometime, but right now I've got a new dog and he's taking up my extra time," I said, placing the white container on the counter.

"Whatcha got now?"

I spent a few moments telling Molly about Sam and his circumstances. "We're still in the getting to know each other phase but so far so good. He's a smart fellow and incredibly strong. He gets along with the other dogs, but I've noticed that tall men still scare him into hiding when they come into the store. He doesn't seem to mind women and children, though, so I believe his fear of men is from his past in the fighting ring. Sallymae's preteens were in here the other day and he was fine with them petting him. He even rolled over and showed his belly."

Molly's phone chirped with a text. She frowned when she read it. "Betsey's already up the mountain at the Lair. Brick's done called a church meeting. Somethin 'bout town and the high school. All the boys are heading that way and I need to get up there. Bye for now, girlfriend!"

I thanked her as she bounced out the door.

Darkness had fallen and I was more than ready to close up, but I left the door open just in case there were some last-minute shoppers. Most of the street had cleared and the band had packed up and left as well. I heard the click-click of claws on the wood floor of my store and sure enough, when I looked behind me, Toto had come through the back room followed by her constant shadow, Sam. I greeted both as they sniffed at the air. Toto liked Betsey's barbecue almost as much as I did and I wasn't surprised when she zoned in on the white box on top of the counter.

"Uh-uh, no you don't. You get yours after I get mine," I stated when she looked at me expectantly. She grunted and flumped down at her usual place. Sam flumped right next to her, pushing her out of the way a bit so he had room on the big doggie bed. She raised her head in annoyance but didn't nip or protest.

I was tidying up my store, putting the displays right and picking up bits of trash that seemed to always come with crowds of people, when I saw Sam jump up at attention and stare avidly at the open front door. He wasn't in an aggressive stance and the hair on his back remained smooth, but he was attentive. I turned and saw little Cody Davis, Blue's youngest child, standing in the doorway, his fingers in his mouth and looking at Sam. He was wearing old jeans that looked too small for him and a grubby T-shirt that was faded and not warm enough for the cool of the night. The fact that my store was still lit up and warm probably drew him here.

"Can I pet your doggie?" he asked, the fingers making his words garbled.

"Sure thing, sweetheart. Just let me throw this bit away and sit with you. He may be nervous meeting new people and it's best if I stay close. Okay?"

His sandy head bobbed a few times and I went to empty my hands of the paper I'd picked up. I sat next to Sam and tucked my skirt over my knees while I beckoned the boy over to me. Sam stayed still and rigid but didn't act scared or aggressive. He sniffed at the small outstretched hand and swiped at it with his tongue. Cody giggled around the digits still in his mouth and finally removed them to smear spit over Sam's head.

"This is Sam and he came from a bad place," I explained, keeping my voice low and easy. I also kept my hands on Sam's back as Cody continued to pet the dog's massive head. "He sometimes growls, but that's only when he's scared."

"Is this a good place?" Cody asked, his pretty blue eyes looking at what was left of Sam's ears.

"Yes, it is," I answered. "Here he gets fed, and petted, and loved on, and has friends to play with."

"Can he play wif me?" Cody piped up, feeling confident enough to plop down next to Sam and me. Toto grunted and moved over a bit more, clearly stating that if she couldn't have any food yet, she wasn't going to pay attention to anyone.

"Maybe," I said vaguely. "Where is your sister?"

As if on cue, Sam let out a *guff*. Michelle appeared in the doorway. "Cody, you were 'posed to stay with me!" she scolded. She was in a short summer dress that had also seen better days and she had a brown paper bag in her hand.

"But it's warm in here," Cody stated, not leaving his place by Sam, his hand still rubbing over the dog's large head. "Smells like flowers and candy."

Michelle came in, wary of Sam but not really afraid of him. She reached out a hand for him to sniff and he treated her to the same sniff and lick he had Cody.

"I smell Gramma's barbecue." She breathed in deeply. Her deep brown eyes matched her father's perfectly and she looked a lot like him. Acted that way too, no-nonsense and straightforward.

"Molly brought me some and there's a lot. Are you hungry? I'm sure your grandmother won't mind if I share with her two favorite grandkids." I spoke lightly. "Are you supposed to be with your mom or your dad tonight?"

I'd seen Blue earlier in uniform, a cell phone glued to his ear as he was at the festival in official capacity. I suspected the kids were supposed to be with their mother, but I needed them to confirm.

"Mommy's busy. Told us to wait near the grocery store, but it got cold," Cody blurted. Michelle was not as forthcoming and stayed quiet. This was unusual, as Betsey had told me once that her granddaughter could wear out an elephant's ear. Maybe she was simply leery of strangers. I hoped it was nothing else.

"Well I don't know your mom real well, but I do know your dad. He's kinda my neighbor. Lives right over there across the street." Both kids looked up at the dark windows above the store.

"Is he home?" Michelle asked hopefully.

"I don't think so, sweetheart. I'm pretty sure he's working tonight," I answered as I closed and locked the front door. "We need to call either him or your mom and let them know where you are. In the meantime, we can dish up some of your grandma's good barbecue. There's plenty for all of us and I've got some chocolate chip cookies Mrs. Pilsner brings for the store. We can break into a few of those as well. What do you think?"

Cody was on board immediately. Michelle was a little slower. "Can we call Daddy instead of Mom?"

"I think that would be fine. What's his number?" I barely got the phone out before she rattled off the information. He picked up in two rings.

"This is Deputy Blue Davis." His voice was rough and sounded tired.

"Hey, Deputy. This is Psalm from Soap-n-stuff. Um, I thought you should know your kids are here with me.

Somehow they got separated from their mother at the festival. They're fine and are welcome to stay here until someone can get them." I hoped I was using the right words.

"Shit!" he barked. I could imagine him running a hand over his face in frustration. "I'm over at the high school dealing with something. It's going to be a while before I can get free and get over there."

"No problem. They can stay here as long as they like. We're going to have some food and hang out for a bit. We'll save a plate for you. Just come to the back door whenever you get here. Okay?" I said reassuringly.

"Yeah. Thanks for this, Psalm. I owe you one. Mind if I speak to Shells for a minute?"

I said goodbye and handed the phone to Blue's daughter. I let them have a private conversation by moving into the back kitchen area and pulling out plates. Cody and Sam followed me.

"Do I hafta eat the slaw?" he asked, standing next to the dog and leaning on him a bit. "Gramma says it's a bestable and we should eat more of them."

I smiled at his pronunciation. "Slaw is mostly made from cabbage, which is a vegetable and yes, your grandma is right about eating them, but I think for tonight I'll leave that up to you whether you eat it or not. Deal?"

"Deal!" he enthused and tucked into the plate I handed him. I added a handful of chips thinking that could be called a "bestable" as well since they were made from potatoes, right?

The other dogs came in from the courtyard and greeted

the children with happy tails moving and lots of barks and licks. Sam stayed next to Cody the entire time, not leaving his side at all. Michelle bonded with Zeke's gentle nature. Maybe the dogs' attention helped her settle because as soon as everyone was fed, the questions started.

"Why do you make soap?" she asked, poking around a shelf of colorful bars.

"I like to make lots of things. Soap is fun because there are lots of colors and scents and patterns I can try. When it gets used up, I can make more."

"Which one is your favorite?"

"I don't think I have one. I like the floral ones and the spicy musk ones too."

"How do you color them?"

The questions and answers went on and on. I thought Michelle was a brilliant little girl, smart, curious, polite, all those qualities that I hoped I would have instilled in a child of my own. I doubted I'd ever get the chance, seeing as my age and my lack of male partner would prohibit that. Adam and I had wanted children, but it wasn't meant to be. I was at peace with it, though. Even if I couldn't have children, I could always enjoy the company of others. Maybe it was time to expand my business and start doing some kid craft classes. I could make space. Afterschool stuff? The idea had possibilities.

A tap on the back door caught my attention. I smiled, thinking Blue had shown up to collect his kids, but instead it was Jonelle and she was furious.

"Where the fuck have you been?" she snapped when

I opened the door. She barged in and slammed her purse down on the counter, knocking over a tray of newly filled lip balm tubes. Her blonde-streaked, black hair was tangled as it bobbed around her neck. She was dressed to the nines in designer skinny jeans and leather boots that matched her leather jacket. "I told you two to stay put at Martin's grocery and I'd be back. Been lookin' all over the street for your little asses!"

Michelle did a complete reversal. Gone was the inquisitive little girl from a few minutes ago. She seemed to collapse in on herself; her eyes fell to the floor and her smiles dried up. Cody shut down completely and moved so close to Sam he was practically climbing the dog.

"Martin's closed. We got cold and came in here to get warm," the little girl said, leaning on Sam's other side.

I noticed the big dog's hackles were now raised and he was standing with his broad shoulders tensed, legs spread in a wide stance, muscles bulging and proud. He was either in attack mode or defense mode. By the way he crowded Cody and Michelle to the side and stood between them and Jonelle, I figured he was in defense. His brown eyes stared intently at the irate woman, as if waiting for a move.

"It was no trouble for the kids to hang here until you arrived, Jonelle. We were about to call you to let you know," I lied. We did call a parent, just not her.

"It stinks in here!" she declared, sniffing and wrinkling her nose. "Smells like someone shit flowers."

I wondered what Miss Emily Post would say about this kind of rude behavior and how to handle it.

"I'm sorry you feel that way," I said, reaching for calm and serenity. *Lavender, bergamot, yling-yling, frankincense,* I chanted in my head, thinking of the scents that reduced stress and eased the mind. Between Sam's escalation and the children's reaction to their mother, someone had to remain in control.

She rolled her eyes and jerked at her bag, pulling out a pack of cigarettes and a lighter. "There's no smoking in the store," I mentioned, still trying to keep calm and even. I was starting to lose that battle.

She lit up anyway and blew a stream of smoke in the air.

"The store owner said there's no smoking in here," a deep voice stated. Blue stood in the back doorway, his khaki uniform rumpled and his face long. The bags under his eyes spoke of a long day and an equally long night.

Jonelle huffed her irritation and snuffed out the cigarette on the counter. My lips thinned. It was a workroom counter and had seen a lot of abuse, but I still didn't like it.

"Well, well, Deputy Dog shows up to save the day. Where the fuck were you earlier when the kids were lost?" she sneered.

"Working a crime scene. Where were you?" he fired right back. "This is your day and your time. Why weren't they with you?"

She flipped her hand in the air and sneered. "I cain't stand over 'em all the time! They's supposed to stay where I told 'em to stay. I cain't help they done run off!"

She tapped out another cigarette before remembering she couldn't smoke in my store. I could tell she was irritated by the constant fidgeting, eyerolls, and huffy breaths she was taking.

"You been drinking tonight?" Blue asked in a low growl.

Jonelle's spine snapped up straight and her perfectly plucked eyebrows came together. "What the fuck, Deputy Dog? I step away for one fuckin' minute to get me one fuckin' beer an' you think I'm drunk? No, I ain't been drinkin' like that! Ain't been smokin' nothin' but cigarettes neither! Ain't been doin' nothin' tonight, asshole! Test me if you want!"

She put her wrists together and held them up in front of her face. "Here ya go! Fuckin' put on them handcuffs, you think you're so smart! Arrest my ass in front o' the kids! I'm sure the judge will look real kindly on that!"

I heard a small whimper and turned to see Cody cowering next to Sam. He was pressed tightly to the dog's flank and had his face buried in the dog's shoulder, his small arms wrapped around Sam's massive neck as far as he could reach. Michelle was on the other side also pressed into the animal, but she had her eyes glued to her ranting mother. *This is not good*, I thought. *These kids do not need to see their parents like this.*

Apparently, Sam thought the same thing. He wasn't moving as Cody clung to him, but he was still standing wide, unmoving, staring at Jonelle with an intensity that was eerie. The hair down the length of his spine was standing straight up. I watched his mouth quiver with the need to snarl and show his deadly teeth.

"I'm not arresting you tonight, Jonelle, but I am going

to report this incident at the next hearing. I have a witness to this behavior this time," Blue stated. I could tell he was angry but he kept it together, probably for his children's sake. One drama queen was bad enough. Adding a king to the mix would be intolerable, even to me.

"Well, you just do that, Deputy Dog!" Jonelle said, sarcasm thick in her voice. "You go fuck yourself while you're at it! Shell 'n' Cody, get your asses to the car!"

The kids stayed put, reluctant to leave. Jonelle lost it. "I SAID MOVE!" she screamed.

Sam answered her with a blood-chilling snarl.

For a moment, her face was filled with fear. "You better keep that fucking dog away from me, bitch! I'll put a goddamn bullet in his head!"

Michelle got up first, petting Sam one last time. Cody kissed the dog's head and said, "Bye, Sam," in a small voice before following his sister. They both moved to hug their father who bent down and whispered in their ears. His words were soft, but his face was hard as granite. I squatted next to Sam and put my hands around his neck in case he decided to go after the kids, or worse, Jonelle. "Stay down," I commanded, hoping that would be enough, though I knew if he really wanted to jump, I didn't have the strength to stop him. I could feel his muscles tremble with the need for action, but he stood rock still, his icy stare still on the raging woman.

"I'll see you in court, asshole!" she yelled before stomping through the door, slamming it hard enough to rattle the ingredient bottles on my shelves. Blue leaned over the counter, both fists balled up, his arms rigid. He was wound just as tight as Sam. The dog started to relax under my fingertips, opening his mouth and panting out some of his stress. I stood up and went to Blue, placing a hand at the middle of his tension-filled shoulders. I still didn't understand why he wouldn't stand up to Jonelle, but I could tell he was fighting for control of his anger and needed support, not criticism. He was a man's man and took a job as a protector. Right now, he was trying to protect his kids, even though it went completely against the grain to let someone walk all over him.

"Fuck!" he exploded when they left the store. He slammed his fists down on the counter, making the bottles rattle again. He was at his last nerve and ready to break.

"I'm so sorry, Blue," I said softly. "I hope I didn't cause this to happen tonight by not calling Jonelle first. The kids were tired and hungry and calling you was the only thing I could think to do about it."

His shoulders lost some of their tightness as he shifted to face me. "Not your fault, Psalm," he stated as he turned and leaned back against the counter. Both hands came up to cover and rub his face. It didn't take a genius to figure out he was exhausted. "It is what it is. Nothing more. I hope the next round in court will end this shit. I'm sorry I couldn't get here earlier. I was at the high school with another drug overdose. Teenage girl this time. There were a bunch of them partying over behind the football bleachers. Ambulance took the kid over to the hospital. Right now, it doesn't look good."

My heart went out to the kid and the family, whoever they were. Blue as well. There was a lot of weight resting on those broad shoulders of his.

"Jonelle and I have a court date in a few weeks over custody and support. I don't know how it's going to go, but until then, I have to adhere to the current arrangement." He made fists again and pounded them against the counter's edge. "Fuck! I can't stand my kids seeing that shit!"

I didn't think about it, I just moved to him and wrapped my arms around him, getting as close as I could, body to body, resting my cheek against his shoulder. I sent mental vibes of comfort and support, hoping some of my Zen calm would reach him. He automatically put his arms around me but hesitated to draw me in.

We stood there for a long time, just holding each other, sharing a human bond. Or at least I thought so. He pushed me away rather abruptly.

"Thanks for taking care of my kids, Psalm," he said gruffly. "Might have to call on you for court. You're a witness now and I need every bit of help I can get." He moved to the doorway as if trying to escape and wouldn't quite meet my eyes.

"Of course, Deputy," I said, feeling a little left out. I crossed my arms in front of my body, trying to keep his heat as long as I could.

Sam huffed again, breaking the awkward moment. He was looking at Blue, his golden eyes serious and his stance still wide, but the hair on his back was flat again.

Blue frowned. "That dog's a fighting dog. He's dangerous.

You're what, maybe a hundred and twenty pounds? You don't have any business trying to handle a dog like that," he said, going into citizen protection mode.

I knelt by Sam and stroked my hands over his short hair. He leaned into me but didn't break the stare down he had going with Blue.

"I think Sam's fine," I said, loving on the large dog. "He's been fitting in nicely, getting along with my other rescues. Come a long way in his life, haven't you, boy?" I spoke directly to Sam, as he had decided Blue was not a problem. He flumped down to the floor to roll over and let me rub his belly. I looked up at Blue from my position on the floor. "Besides, I'm sure you saw how he was ready to defend Cody and Michelle. He may have been a fighting dog at one time but now he's a pack protector."

Blue just grunted. "It's been a long night. I'm heading out. Don't forget to lock up behind me." He moved to the back door, then paused long enough to turn and mutter, "Thanks again," before leaving and closing the door with a soft click. I finished petting the lounging animal and then moved to do as Blue had bid. As I was locking the door, I caught sight of Blue coming out of the back alleyway on his bike and heading up the street. I sighed and turned to my workroom, still restless myself from the night's events. Hm... soap, or maybe some new candles?

CHAPTER 7

The Lair was in full party mode when Blue drove up on his Harley. It was late and most people of his town were down for the night. Here, the lodge was hopping with music, bikers, and hangarounds. Blue parked his bike at the end of a long line of them and entered into the welcoming chaos. The Dragon Runners members were obvious, dressed in their distinctive cuts with the flaming green symbol sewn on the back. The spine of the beast represented a jagged curved road superimposed along a mountain. This was the Tail of the Dragon, a long and dangerous road with a long history of being both a biker's wet dream to ride and his worst nightmare. Many lives had been lost on that road, one of them just a year ago. Joker, a former brother, had betrayed the club and kidnapped another member's old lady to try and make an escape. This didn't end well for him, as he lost control on one of the roughest curves and paid for it with his life in a fiery crash. The old lady, Kat, was pushed out just before the car flew over the cliff edge and suffered injuries so severe she wasn't expected to make it. She did, however, and was now happily married to Mute, the club's sergeant-at-arms and enforcer.

Kat was behind the bar at the far end of the Lair's great room, serving drinks. His mother Betsey and her friends Molly and Tambre were sitting around the bar on high stools that were more chainsaw art than seats. They were a throwback memory of the old Rivers Edge bar and resembled the rear end of horses. From the back, it looked like they were sitting on horses' asses.

A loud chorus of "Bloooooo!" rang out as he entered and walked across the floor. Some high fives and hand slaps later, he was sitting with several club members and had a cold beer in his hand. The noise around him was comforting and familiar. He'd grown up in this place and had watched its transformation from a one-percenter criminal group to a legit business group during his early childhood. The Dragon Runners still did things their own way and had their own code of right and wrong, but they stayed within the confines of the law—or at least appeared to most of the time. Blue knew there were some activities that pushed the limit and some that were illegal, but he also believed that there was sometimes a difference between what was law, what was right, and what was true justice.

Betsey came over and hugged him. "Hey, darlin', you doin' all right? Your daddy's up with Taz and Cutter playing poker if you wanna join in?"

His mother was amazing, and it was hard to believe she was a grandmother.

"I wish I could, but I can't afford poker with Cutter right now. You know he cheats."

They both laughed.

"Been better." He jammed a hand over his tired face. "Jonelle lost the kids at the festival tonight. They wandered into the soap store on Main and the owner called me."

Betsey blinked at the news. "Psalm's place? I know it. She makes the best wrinkle cream in the world. Are Shells and Cody okay? Where are they?"

"I was at the high school dealing with another overdose. Jonelle showed up at the store just before I did and we had a fight in front of the kids again. I had to let them go with her, but it about killed me."

He took a deep swallow of the beer. The chatter continued around him, but he felt alone and isolated.

"I think she's using again, Mama, but I haven't been able to catch her yet."

Betsey clicked her tongue. "I'm so sorry, sweetheart. I saw 'em when I was workin' the booth, but that bitch wouldn't let 'em come see me. If I'd known them kids was alone, I'd a brought 'em up here till you got off work."

One of the club members got up from the couch to make room for her and she slid into the space. "Somethin's gonna need to be done about her, Blue. Them kids ain't doing well. Michelle's getting real quiet and that ain't normal for her. Cody's 'bout scared of everything and gettin' worse. When's the court hearing?"

"Three weeks from yesterday," Blue told her, jamming a hand over his face. "I still need to find a better place to live.

No judge is going to allow me overnights while I'm living in that shit hole."

"You can always come back here," Betsey whispered. "The kids would always be safe and have a ready-made family with lots of uncles and aunts. You know the judge will think twice and then some before messin' with the Dragon Runners."

Blue burped lightly. "I know that, Mama, but if I did, I'd go back to being Brick and Betsey's son instead of Blue Davis, Deputy of Bryson City. I need to be out and be my own man with my own name. If it comes down to brass tacks, I'll do what I have to do to keep my kids safe, including come back here, but unless something goes really bad, I need to do my own thing. A man is no man unless he can stand on his own two feet and take care of his family."

Betsey blew out a pshhhhhtt between her red-painted lips and scowled at him. "Yeah, well, sometimes that man needs to accept a little help from time to time from his mama or his woman. Was Psalm there when Jonelle pitched her hissy fit?"

"Yeah, she was there. I'll call on her for the court hearing if I need to." Blue was exhausted and could feel his energy draining from his body. "I'm gonna crash here tonight, Mama. I'm wiped. Can you tell Dad I want to talk to him in the morning about this new drug shit coming through town? Had another kid OD tonight. I need to see if the Runners have any idea of what's going on."

Betsey hesitated. This was a clash between worlds and had to be played right. "Your daddy and the club ain't got nothing to do with the drugs running through town. You know that, Blue. They's just as bothered by it as anyone else and mean to put a stop to it like you do, but you know the club's got a different way of coming to justice. Might be your daddy won't share everything he knows."

"I know, Ma, but I gotta ask anyway. I'm grasping at straws and feel like it's only a matter of time before I have another damaged or dead kid from this stuff. We'll cross the next bridge when we get there." He got up from the couch and hugged his mother goodnight.

She hugged him back. "Sleep well, son. You always got a place here. Love you."

Blue settled in the room that was kept for him in the living quarters that took up the majority of the second floor. The sounds of the club's active night were faint as he stripped his uniform off and climbed into the queen-sized bed. He reached out to the nightstand and remembered his soap bar was still in his apartment. He'd gotten into the habit of smelling it every night and found himself missing the ritual. He had showered with it occasionally and found the scent did cling to him during the day, but he used a different soap most of the time as he wanted to make that bar last as long as possible. He knew he could always buy another one but for some reason, it was important to him to keep this one. Blue closed his eyes and called up the lavender fragrance in his memory. Even from miles away, he could smell the soap's calming scent and was able to fall asleep.

CHAPTER 8

Sunday was my favorite day of the week as it was my only real day off. Sometimes I'd sleep in if the dogs let me. Sleeping in meant I could stay in bed until six or seven, so for most people, it wouldn't seem to be a luxury, but I'd learned to appreciate those extra few hours. Sunday was also Pamper Night. I got to take a long two-tub bath with my Kindle, use a body scrub, try a new face mask, shave my legs, groom my eyebrows, deep condition my hair, and whatever girly girl indulgence I wanted. A two-tub bath was when I filled the tub with water as hot as I liked, lounged in it until it cooled, then drained and filled it again. Some people may have called it waste. I called it therapy.

Some Sunday mornings I spent with my parents, taking the dogs out to their farm and letting them run in the large fields and wooded areas around their house. I used to be afraid they'd get lost, but they never wandered so far they couldn't hear my call. I had the opinion that their lives had been rough enough that they knew they'd won the doggie lottery when they came to live with me. Sometimes I went to church with my parents, but I was just as content to go to their house in the early afternoon and hang out, messing around in Mom's kitchen or seeing what new project Dad had started.

This Sunday was no exception as the snuffling and whining started at six thirty and I dragged myself out of bed to let the dogs out for potty time. Sam stayed right by me, still in protection mode, and was reluctant to go outside with the rest to take care of business, but Toto pushed him into it. She was the best dog ever!

An hour later, I had everyone packed up and in the truck, heading out of town to my parents' farm. As I drove off, I noticed Blue's lights were off. By this time every morning he was always up. I was concerned a bit, but Blue was a grown man and I was sure he was okay and somewhere safe. I had wondered from time to time where he went at night on his motorcycle, but also knew it was really none of my business as he always came home. Maybe he was really there and sleeping in. Last night had been rough on him and the kids, and my heart twinged for all three of them. Jonelle could kiss my ass!

My parents lived in an old farmhouse that sat in the back half of an open field. The house had been in my family for generations but had been modernized over the years. It still sported the same square boxy look of most farmhouses in the area, with a large living room and eat-in kitchen on the bottom floor, three large bedrooms on the second floor, and a root cellar underneath. Electricity was added a long time ago, but the kerosene lamp sconces were still on the wall. The house had been updated with new siding and roof, and recently my parents had the cable buried instead of draping down the long driveway. Dad said he hadn't liked the look of having all those tall poles obstructing his view. There was running water courtesy of a well pump and made hot by a propane tank. The kitchen still had the ancient woodstove my grandmother used, and my mother preferred to cook on it for the most part, although there was an electric one in the corner. I'd always loved the combination of traditional and modern the house and my parents represented. It was funny to see my dad stoking a fire in the woodstove that heated the living room and then settle himself in his La-Z-Boy at night to watch sports through satellite on a big flat-screen TV.

The farm had been a working one for years, growing burly leaf tobacco at one time for commercial use. Now some of the large fields were leased by other farmers as my dad was retired from working the land as much. He still had the fields around the house grow wild for hay and had it cut and baled already, and he also maintained a rather large garden, growing corn, potatoes, pole beans, tomatoes, and other vegetables. He was rather thin, but he was spry and always full of life. It was hard for him to sit still and he liked to be working on something every day. The garden kept him busy, as the produce from it fed them, me, and several other families. Mom called him the Energizer Bunny.

Mom was old-school as well, getting homemade cheese, milk, and sausage from neighbors. She kept a few chickens for fresh eggs but didn't like to use them for meat. Sometimes the dogs would chase them around the house, but they had learned the hard way that Speckles, the rooster, was rather defensive of his territory. She still made her own soap with the same recipe her mother taught her using lard or rendered fat from venison. Her bars were plain and functional, which suited the needs of the farm. I used the same base recipe for some of my stuff but had expanded and changed it over the years and never used animal fat.

I pulled into the parking area right outside the house and saw my dad coming out of the woodshed with his arms full of logs for the kitchen fire. I waved as I opened the back and let the dogs jump out. They greeted my dad with doggie smiles and barks, their butts moving as rapidly as their tails. Buddy and Zeke took off after Speckles and Dion explored the closest bush. Toto greeted my dad with her head-butting hug against his leg.

He bent over, scratching at her graying ears. "Whatcha got there, little missy? A new boarder?"

Sam had taken up his usual spot sitting on his haunches next to me.

"This is Sam, Dad, and yes, he's new. Just came last week from Virginia. Remember that raid earlier this year on the dogfighting ring? This is one of the fighters."

"Huh," my dad grunted. "Don't look like no mean dog. Least not now. I'm sure you know what you're doin'. You always had the soft touch with critters. Come on. Let's go up to the house. Your ma'll be wantin' to see you."

Mom was bustling around the kitchen, the salty tang of bacon and the sweet smell of fresh bread wafting in the air. She pulled a crusty brown loaf out of the electric oven, then turned and flipped the crispy strips of meat on the woodstove. The flat iron griddle had been the one my grandmother had used and was still in service. Nothing tasted better than bacon and buckwheat cakes cooked on that griddle.

"Hello, sweetheart. Breakfast'll be ready soon. Gotta finish the cakes, though. Grab them bowls over there and start dipping the cookie dough. Ain't gonna make services today. Got too much to finish this morning. The Addison family had a death this week. The oldest boy passed on. Big shame. He was only seventeen. They say he got ahold a some drug been goin 'round over to t'the high school. Made his heart go too fast for his body. Emma Jean is beside herself and I cain't blame her. Buck was her firstborn and was looking at a full scholarship over to NC State for football. She's just plumb done in."

I dipped cookie dough into mounds on the old flat cookie sheets. The fragrance of ginger and other spices drifted up to my nose. "There was another drug overdose last night at the festival. Deputy Davis said it happened at the high school as well, but I don't know who it was this time. Just that it was a girl. I'm sure you'll hear soon enough." I sighed. "I hope he can find out where this stuff is coming from and put an end to it."

"Lord have mercy!" Mom declared, shaking her short white hair. She was just as much a firecracker as my dad, always working at a project or doing something for somebody. "Betsey and Brick done raised a good boy. I never understood how he could marry that no 'count Jonelle Mason. She had good folks too, with good raisin' but Lord knows she turned out a disappointment. She's done took up with some other no 'count according to her mama."

I smiled as I listened to my mother rattle on about other relatives and families, people's health, happenings at the church, and other gossip bits. Her hands stayed busy, pouring batter onto the well-seasoned griddle and flipping the bubbling pancakes. She was just as much an Energizer Bunny as my dad.

"Call your daddy. Cakes are done."

I stepped out to the covered porch, put two fingers in my mouth, and blasted a short but loud whistle. I saw my dad start toward the house, accompanied by my dogs. My mom had taught me how to do this years ago but could still out-whistle me in both volume and duration.

We sat down at the well-worn table. Dad said grace and we started in on the morning feast. The dogs sat around him, waiting for handouts. It was an age-old game my parents played. My dad would sneak bits to the dogs and Mom would scold him for it, but she would do the same when he wasn't looking.

Mom looked at Sam, who was plastered next to me. "That one's got a story, don't he?" she remarked. "Looks like he's been rode hard and put up wet but seems real watchful. Gonna be trouble, you think?"

"No, I don't think so." I explained Sam's history of fighting and abuse. I also described his protective attitude around Cody and Michelle.

Mom nodded. "Makes sense. He may come from a bad place, but he's a good dog. Got a lot of loyalty in him. You can tell by the way he stays guardin' next to you."

We spent the rest of the morning and afternoon working in the kitchen and playing with the dogs. Sam did finally join in and played with the other dogs, chasing the balls my dad threw and wrestling. They were tired puppies when I loaded them and several bags of fresh vegetables in the truck to go home. On the way, I got a call from Dr. Jackson. Someone had seen a photo of Buddy on the adoption site and was interested in meeting him. I asked her to text me the number since I was driving and I would call them later to set up a time to meet next week. Hopefully Buddy would find his forever home.

As I pulled into my narrow driveway, I noticed Blue's lights were on. He was home and I hoped he had a good day. I knew I needed the space of my parents' place out of town from time to time to recharge my batteries. I was sure he did too.

I got the dogs settled and started my pamper night. First, a hair mask of a bunch of oils, wild honey, and egg yolks. It was a messy affair I'd wash out later, but the deep conditioning made my hair soft and full. Once my hair was wrapped in a plastic cap and warmed towel, I put on a deep clay face mask. It was a powerful skin tightener as well as detoxifier. Sam stared at me with wide eyes because of the dark gray gook smeared on my face. Next, I filled the tub with the first round of water and threw in a bath bomb of lemongrass and ginger. The sphere spun as it fizzed in the water and filled the air with its citrusy scent. I had a plate of mom's ginger cookies and a big cup of decaf coffee sitting on the side table next to the tub. Heaven!

The heat of the water was soothing and I relaxed into its depths. I was starting to think about Christmas soaps, lotions, and new scent blends when my phone beeped. I looked at the screen and was surprised to see it was a text from Blue.

Blue: I saved your number when you called me about the kids at the street festival. I hope that's ok. I wanted to thank you again for your help with them. I was not in a good place the other night and hope I didn't offend you. Thanks for being there.

Butterflies erupted in my stomach at the message. I dried my fingers and texted back.

Me: No problem. They are welcome here anytime. How is the girl from the festival? Still at the hospital?

Blue: No. She passed a few hours ago. Doctor said there was just too much damage to her heart.

This was bad news. Even though I didn't know the girl or her family, I still felt their sorrow.

Me: I'm so sorry. I'm sure her family is devastated. How are you holding up?

I wasn't sure what else to say. I held the phone a few more minutes.

Blue: It's rough but I'm dealing, or at least I'm trying. What are you up to tonight?

I held my breath as those stupid butterflies shifted in my stomach. Should I be honest and tell him I was in the tub with a clay mask on my face and oily goop in my hair? Um… no. I finally texted back thinking I didn't need to tell him all that I was doing.

Me: It's my pamper night so I'm lounging in my tub and reading a book.

Blue: Pamper night?

Me: Yup. All the girly things we women like to do that will remain a mystery.

Blue: Like bubble baths and facials?

Me: How do you know about facials?

Blue: I have a mother who buys that stuff from you. Her two best friends do also.

Me: I see.

I was trying to think of something, anything to text in response when his next message came through.

Blue: I meant what I said about going to court for me in a few weeks. I could use the help if you're willing.

Me: Again, no problem, Deputy. I just hope the kids can get through this mess. They're the real victims. :(

I waited for a few minutes for another reply. Maybe calling his kids victims wasn't a good idea but it was accurate in my mind. Poor Cody was so confused and scared. I wished there was a way Sam could be with him. He seemed to bond with the boy and act more as a protector.

My phone dinged in my hand again.

Blue: Call me Blue. You got boxes tomorrow? Coffee tomorrow morning?

Those butterflies twirled through my stomach.

Me: Always have boxes. See you then, Blue. Sleep well

The bath water was getting colder now and I had been planning on a two-tub night but decided I was done. The water gurgled down the drain as I slathered on a moisturizing body butter. Mom always called it my hippie cream, but I called it my fool's cream as the oils were known to firm skin and reduce or eliminate wrinkles. I wasn't an old person and I didn't mind aging, but that didn't mean I wasn't going to put up a fight. Besides, it was one of my best sellers. Betsey usually bought three jars at a time.

I put on my favorite lounging pants, ones that were made by Eva. They were a silky soft cotton in a muted pale blue. I added a white tank top. Sticking my nose back in my book would be the perfect end to a perfect day, but that was not going to happen. Instead, I read Blue's texts over and over again. There was nothing in them that was any more than friendly. The same kind of exchange you'd have with a cousin or a friend. Yet I was still stirred up. Restless. Bleh! I could feel another long night coming on. I'd been having too many of them lately and I knew it would catch up with me at some point, but unless I wanted to start taking sleeping medication, I'd keep working it out on my own.

I stood up, put on my fluffy robe and slippers, and decided to go down to the workroom to putter. Perhaps my brain would slow down enough to sleep. Toto and Sam raised their heads from the bed and watched me. Toto grunted and settled back down, as she was used to this occurrence. Sam got up and followed me to the workroom, settling on the doggie bed there to keep me company and to guard. I talked to him as I worked just to have a bit of noise.

"Got a big order in for bath bombs. Remember that woman who nearly cleaned me out at the festival? One hundred assorted pikake, jasmine, rose, and gardenia. The woman wants them as wedding favors and in colors that match her bridesmaids."

I pulled out the big tubs of baking soda and citric acid and set several mixing bowls on the table.

"I think she's got a flower theme going on, but what a mix of flowers! I hope no one in the wedding party has any allergies."

I snapped on some short latex gloves to protect my hands from the drying effects of the citric acid. I measured the powders, added a bit of sweet almond oil, and started stirring the mixture together. I chattered at Sam, who thumped his tail at my voice to let me know he was still listening, but otherwise didn't move or even open his eyes.

Light pink for the pikake, lavender for the jasmine, yellow for the rose, and white for the gardenia; I mixed the colors in the giant bowls and began pressing the bombs into plastic snap-together molds. This was tougher than it looked and I knew my hands and arms would be sore tomorrow from the effort. Scoop, press, scoop some more, force together and snap, repeat. I was in the zone and starting to feel myself relax. I needed to finish the bombs as the ingredients were already mixed, but I was feeling myself starting to drift, finally ready to sleep. Hopefully, I'd sleep well.

The knock on my door was unexpected and startling. Even Sam jumped a bit. I looked through the door's window and spotted none other than Blue looking in on me. Damn, those butterflies were still awake and had morphed into buzzing bees.

CHAPTER 9

After his text with Psalm, Blue grabbed a bottle of beer from his tiny fridge and took a long swallow. The ease he felt from the brief digital conversation left him rather quickly. The day couldn't have been shittier and he was feeling every minute of it. The last few weeks had left him restless and edgy. This was supposed to be his day off with his kids, but he'd been called away on an emergency and both his parents were out of town on a run to the club's newest campground acquisition. He'd had to drop the kids off at Jonelle's place earlier than he wanted and she had given him shit for it. Another high school kid had hyped up on some bad drug and was running up and down the aisles of the local Walmart naked with a hunting knife, slashing at whoever he could get near. By the time he got there, the kid had collapsed into a seizure, his heart unable to keep up with the drug. He was currently at the hospital in a coma and not expected to last much longer. With the girl from the festival passing and this new likely casualty, Blue was on a constant edge, frustrated, and feeling helpless to do his job.

Blue held the bottle loosely in his fingers and ran the cool glass over his tired forehead. This was the fourth or fifth kid to overdose, and the second in the last twenty-four hours he'd had to deal with. So far, all of them had died, which you'd think would deter anyone from using this new drug. He'd spend some time this morning talking to his dad about the problem. Brick was trying to find out more about the sudden drug influx as well. Too many people made the assumption it was the Dragon Runners who were bringing the stuff in, and Brick had fought too long and hard to clean up his club and keep his people safe to let it backslide. The club now owned a number of profitable and legitimate businesses that kept its members employed and very well off. No need to mess that up. Brick was just as concerned about this new meth-type drug.

Jonelle had also come after him again, claiming if he wasn't spending his court-allotted time with the kids, then he shouldn't be allowed to have that time. They were headed back to court soon and she was looking for anything to use against him. She'd taken the kids in the house without a word and later called him to yell at him at the same time he was at the hospital watching a thin teenage boy fighting for his life and losing. At least she hadn't lost her shit in front of the kids. Well, he hoped not, but he had no control over what she did or said after she hung up on him. He imagined she trash-talked him to their children, and soon that would take a toll. They had seen too much happen between their parents already and Blue was concerned about the damage this would cause.

Michelle seemed to be two kids in one body. Sometimes he saw glimpses of the cute six-year-old she was supposed to be, like when she was grilling someone new with questions. Other times she was quiet as a mouse, reserved and still, afraid to move and being extremely cautious in choosing her words. Almost fearful. Cody was merely a shadow of himself. Something was going on with both kids and he felt it was more than the nasty battle between their parents. He couldn't put a finger on it and when he talked to his kids, they shut down.

Shit with work; shit with Jonelle; Christ almighty, even shit with his daughter. He felt the entire weight of the planet on his shoulders and his knees were starting to buckle.

Fuck! He leaned against the window of his shitty apartment overlooking the street and rubbed the sweating bottle against his brow. So many people depending on him to stay in control, stay on top of things, fix everyone's problems, and somehow remain sane. Jonelle's money demands and the upcoming court battle, the sudden influx of meth substances in the small town, whatever was happening with his kids. It was too much at times, and more than once he'd thought about just gathering his stuff, loading his truck, and leaving. But that wasn't an option. He could never leave his kids or his family.

A light came on in the soap shop across street. Psalm was up and messing around with her soaps and lotions again. His thoughts drifted to her gentle eyes and soothing voice. He closed his own eyes as he recalled her words from earlier in the week. Many of the other store owners had given him shit for the new council rule, and Psalm had been upset too, but had not blamed or ranted at him for it. In fact, she had given him a gift and thanked him for doing his job. Her words had been "I appreciate you for it." For a moment, he had felt good. She'd also taken care of his kids when they were in need. Michelle had been fascinated with the stuff in the workroom. Cody had clung to that monster dog like a prickly burr, taking comfort in that massive animal.

She'd hugged him when he needed it the most, giving him the human contact he hadn't realized he was craving. He'd felt that connection even through the text conversation just a little while ago. She couldn't really take his burdens, but she seemed to understand them and was willing to stand up for him and with him. Christ Almighty, he missed having someone in his life.

Without knowing how he got there, he found himself at her back door, looking at her bustling in her workshop. She was wearing a white robe and pale blue lounge pants, mixing powders and pressing them into two halves of a plastic ball.

His hand came up and knocked lightly at the door and his heart pounded as she glanced up, startled, and then smiled with that slow blink of hers. She unlocked the door and gentle floral scents hit his nostrils. He inhaled deeply, his mind growing calmer just being in her presence.

"Hello, Blue. Can't sleep?" Her sweet voice rushed over him like a blanket.

"Noticed your light and thought I'd come check on you.

Make sure you're okay." He fumbled as he picked up a bottle of… something. A glance at the label told him it was bergamot essential oil. He brought it to his nose and sniffed at it so he wouldn't have to meet her eyes. If he looked into their deep bluish-gray depths, he would want to drown in them.

"That's very sweet. I know it's been rough in town lately with this drug problem, and you've had a lot on your plate. I'm really sorry this mess is happening and you're having to deal with it. I feel terrible for the families of those kids. I can't imagine what they're going through," she said while she whisked a bright pink concoction in a large mixing bowl. She shoveled a handful of the powder into another round mold and pressed the two halves together, forming a perfect pink ball. "I'm sure it's not a picnic in the park to deal with Jonelle either."

He let out an ironic sound. "If you only knew."

She placed the filled mold on a tray with a bunch of other ones in pastel colors. "I know you're a good man going through a really rough patch right now. I wish there was something I could do to help you, but I expect this is one fight you have to see through on your own." She looked up at him. "If you need to share a bit just to get stuff off your chest, feel free to talk or text anytime. I promise I won't be telling people everything I know."

"I'll keep that in mind." Blue fingered one of the filled plastic balls. "What are these?" he asked. He wasn't ready to go but couldn't stay. Getting his thoughts and worries off his chest sounded like heaven, but he didn't want to add his burdens to anyone else's. Her nearness made him think of things he had no business thinking.

"Bath bombs," she answered, pressing another one into a mold. "They've gotten real popular. They fizz up and fill the tub with oils and fragrance when you get a chance to wind down from the day in a tub of warm water. At least that's what my tagline for these pieces is going to be. What do you think?"

"I think if you can solve the world's problems by taking a bath, I'll jump in and never get out."

She laughed and placed the new ball on the tray to join the others. "Baths, bath bombs, good-smelling stuff, none of that will solve anything, but at least it can help you get away for a bit. These are scented with gardenia. Too floral for a man like you, but I'll make a batch with a cedar and lavender scent. More spicy and masculine."

He didn't tell her he didn't have a bathtub in his apartment and probably wouldn't use it if he did. "Thanks."

She treated him to his favorite smile.

He fumbled a bit with a bottle of tangerine oil, feeling the need to leave still but not wanting to. The plastic ball mold crunched softly as she pressed it together, the only sound in the room.

"I'd better leave you to your—uh, bomb making," he finally said, not able to come up with any other excuses to stay.

He turned to go.

"Just a moment, Blue." He watched as she took off her gloves and wiped her hands on the dishtowel she had draped over her shoulder. She came to stand in front of him and, without hesitation, enfolded him in her arms. He could feel calm, accepting peace coming from her and it nearly sent him to his knees. He inhaled the gentle fragrance wafting from her hair and it was all he could do to not to bury his nose in the soft blonde mass. The unconditional support was something he craved more than air and needed more than water. He gave himself that for a moment, feeling the crush of her breasts against his chest and the brush of her hands as they stroked over his back.

He pushed her away abruptly, a little rougher than he meant to, and didn't look at her face as he hardened his own.

"What are you doing, Psalm?"

She blinked in surprise at his hard tone. "Um… I was—just giving you a hug."

"Why?" The word lashed out like a whip.

"I—uh, thought you may need one," she answered, confusion on her face and in her voice. She folded in a bit, crossing her arms in front of herself and holding in whatever she had been offering to him.

He needed to set some boundaries, mostly for himself. "Right now, I don't need anything from you but your testimony in court. Might not even need that if I play my cards right. I appreciate your help with my kids, but don't go reading into something that ain't there."

"I understand, Blue. I really didn't mean anything other than to give you a hug. I'm sorry. I'll still be glad to help you with the kids if you need me."

Blue felt like a dick. Psalm was such a gentle, giving

woman and was only trying to be supportive. He pinched his eyes between his thumb and index finger and let out a huge sigh. "Look, Psalm, I'm sorry I just jumped your shit. I'm really tired and have a lot going on, but it doesn't mean I should take it out on you. I need as many friends as I can get right now. Can we just leave it at that?"

Her smile reappeared and she slowly blinked. "Friends is good. I can definitely do that for you. Call me, text me, whatever you need. Deal?"

"Deal," he agreed. Suddenly, he was completely drained and ready to fall asleep on his feet. Coming over to Psalm's place did indeed make him feel calmer and better in control. Maybe her hugs weren't such a bad idea. He had to leave before he started something he couldn't finish.

"Listen, I'm gonna head home. Lock up behind me and don't stay up too much longer yourself. You're probably worn out from the weekend, and tomorrow is a workday for both of us. Coffee shop?"

Her smile got even brighter and Blue's breath stilled in his chest.

"Sure thing, Blue. See you later."

Blue left and went back to his dismal apartment. The place wasn't well insulated and there was a chill in the air. He stripped and crawled between the cold sheets, his mind still confused but at least easy enough to sleep. He glanced over at the steadily shrinking bar of soap, picked it up, and inhaled its scent deep into his lungs. He stood up, took the bar into the bathroom, and placed it on the shower shelf before returning to bed.

CHAPTER 10

Monday morning was tough. I only had a few hours of fitful sleep before I had to start my day. After Blue had left, I sat on the counter for a while. Sam had looked up at me with his big gold eyes, his ears forward, asking if I was all right. I was and I wasn't. I wondered why he didn't bark or anything when Blue spoke roughly to me. Maybe he thought Blue was the pack alpha?

Deputy Davis. I have to call him that. He can't be Blue to me. He has to be Deputy Davis.

I dragged myself out of bed, more reluctant than ever to get up and start my day. Toto was moving stiffer this morning. Her arthritis was getting worse and there would come a point when the daily pills wouldn't work anymore to ease her pain. I truly dreaded that time.

The rest of the dogs were their usual selves, oblivious to the woes of the world and ready to play. It did help my mood to be surrounded by wagging tails and wiggling butts all vying for scratches. Today, I had to set up a meeting with

Buddy's potential family, a set of parents with two young boys who liked Buddy's patchwork face.

I went through my routine, but I didn't look through my window to check for Blue doing his.

Deputy. Deputy. Deputy, I chanted in my head while I was putting on my makeup for the day, hoping to break the habit of calling him Blue. That was too personal and I needed the distance, especially after last night. I looked down at Sam, who was watching me at my vanity table.

"Fat chance of that, eh boy?" I said to him, scratching behind a stumpy ear. His response was to open his mouth and pant a bit. He lifted a paw to rest on my hand as if saying "there, there. tiny human."

I shook myself. *Stop it, Psalm! The man has enough to deal with without you adding an old moony high school crush to the mix. It was a one-time thing a long time ago so enjoy it for that, but don't add to the man's burdens by expecting anything more.*

He was at the coffee shop just before I got there and had two coffees in his hands waiting for me. I smiled and took the paper cup with a gentle thank-you. I was thinking of ordering a double espresso shot for the extra caffeine, but I wasn't going to complain at having a handsome man buy my morning cup.

"Good morning, Deputy."

"Mornin', Psalm. Thought I said last night you can call me Blue."

I took a sip of the delicious brew and let it roll across my tongue. Pam was a coffee master!

"I think since you're in uniform, I should probably call you Deputy. I wouldn't want anyone to get the idea I get preferential treatment."

Blue took a sip from his own cup and one corner of his mouth raised. "I'll still ticket you if you mess up, Psalm, but maybe you'll pay with somethin' besides money."

My insides quivered at his reply and I was at a loss for words until he opened his mouth again.

"I may charge you soap bars and those bath things. Christmas is comin' and I know Mama likes bubble baths."

I smiled and dropped my eyes to the floor.

"Mind if I ask you something personal?"

His question had me looking up again.

"How come your parents named you Psalm? I remember you were the only one in high school with that name. It's nice, but it ain't common."

I smiled. "I don't mind answering. Mom wanted a Bible name and shuffled through a bunch of them. Esther, Hannah, Naomi, Mary, lots of them but couldn't choose. When she went into labor with me, she was reading in the book of Psalms and decided it was a sign that was what she was supposed to name me."

He drank more coffee and nodded. "Makes sense to me. Unique and pretty-sounding. Suits you."

The heat of a blush crept across my face and I dropped my eyes again, making an acknowledging *hmm* sound.

"You got stuff to ship?"

I nodded while taking another healthy swig of my drink. "Every day. Now that I have the website, I get a lot of online business. It's a pain, but it's a nice problem to have."

He grunted, tilted his head, and swallowed the last of his coffee. I watched his throat work with fascination.

"Let's get to it then."

With Blue's help, I made my shipping run and started my work day. Today, I wore maroon leggings, flat-heeled black leather boots, and a long-sleeved printed tunic. I'd brushed my freshly treated hair out and let it hang loose. My makeup was colored to blend in with the colors of my tunic, but I did add a little eye glitter to the mix. A girl needs a little sparkle every now and then. The days were still fairly warm but would be getting colder soon. Tourists would be coming through the area all the way up until New Year's Eve, which was over three months away, but the main traffic of the season was just about finished.

I decided it was time to get my Christmas scents ready. Because cold process soap can take so long to fully cure and I usually had a butt-ton of orders to fill, I had to start way ahead and guess on how much of each seasonal soap I needed to make. Some of the stores that bought from me wholesale sent me a list of what they wanted and how much. This helped a lot. Some stores simply ordered what they wanted at the time and reordered when they ran out. This didn't help any, but so far I'd been able to fulfill all my orders including my own store.

I was layering thickened soap batter in several ten-pound loaf molds when the bell rang.

"Welcome to Soap-n-stuff! I'll be with you in a moment!"

I called out.

"No problem, darlin'. We're just browsin' right now, but I need some more of my wrinkle cream." I closed my eyes and wished I could melt into the floor. It was Betsey.

Tambre was with her and both women were looking at the newest pottery from a local artist. Tambre had bought several pieces from this collection and said she wanted to add more when the artist fired his next batch. Lucky timing, right?

"Hi, Betsey, hi, Tambre. I see you found the new stuff. He just finished last week and this lot was brought in a few days ago. Fabulous, aren't they?" I poured the final layer into the soap mold. This was a popular scent I made year-round, but it sold like hot cakes at Christmas. The scent was a tropical fruity one using mango, coconut, and banana, called Monkey Farts. Kids loved it for the seminaughty name and adults loved the novelty. It really didn't matter what the appeal was, I just knew how much sold during the holidays and my stock was going down fast. I layered the soap in kind of a banana cream pie look. Brown layer on the bottom, then yellow, then a thin tangerine, then white on top with a fluffed whipped look to it. To further the monkey idea, I piped little bananas and oranges all over the top with soap in a pastry bag. I thought it was cute and my customers did as well. This was the first of twenty pounds I would be making of this particular soap today.

"You doin' all right? I heard about Jonelle comin' in here the other night," Betsey asked, not waiting but jumping right in. "I wanted to thank you for takin' care of my grandkids.

They's had it rough lately with their mama and daddy fightin'. I wish I could do more, but Blue's gotta do his own thing. He's just as stubborn as his daddy."

She picked up a Give Me Your Heart soap that was scented with pikake, jasmine, and a touch of vanilla. The soap had a bright pink heart in the middle and was surrounded by lavender and white layers. Another good seller of mine.

"Shells told me about this one. Says it's her favorite. Probably for the pink. That kid's wild about pink. She's a tomboy most of the time. Don't mind gettin' dirty and roughing around on the four wheelers up at the Lair and such, but loves the girly stuff too." Betsey sighed as she inhaled the scent and pulled three of the colorful soaps from the bin. I made a mental note to check my stock and put that design in the production lineup this week.

"Damn shame what them kids is goin' through," she continued as she moved to the counter and watched me pipe little orange dots next to the yellow arcs on top of the soap loaf I was working on. Tambre was still looking at the pottery, lifting several pieces to move to the counter.

"I'm very sorry all this is happening to them. I'm sorry for their daddy and mom, too," I responded, finishing up the piping and putting the bag to the side to take off my rubber gloves and wipe off my sweaty hands. The gloves were necessary in working with raw soap batter as it was still very caustic and would continue to saponify for the next twenty-four hours. Necessary, but rather uncomfortable.

"Is that Sam over there?" Betsey asked, lifting and pointing her chin behind me. I turned to see the bulky dog come through the workroom door from the courtyard. He came and stood next to me, peering silently up at the strangers.

"Yes, this is Sam." I bent and scratched him behind his ears as he leaned into my legs. "He's a recent rescue. I guess Cody mentioned him?"

"Oh Lord, yes! That boy was on the phone this mornin' talkin' up a storm about that dog. He forgot all about bein' scared and waitin' for his mama at the festival. All he could say was Sam this and Sam that. Shells talked about him too, sayin' he's a big one and he done scared Jonelle some."

Her eyes went back to the behemoth sitting next to me. "I guess she was right. He's a little intimidatin', ain't he?"

I laughed lightly. "I suppose he could be, but he hasn't shown any aggression at all. Well, not to me or anyone else except for Jonelle. I think it was because she was yelling and arguing. He didn't blink when Blue, um, came by that night."

Somehow, I didn't think I needed to tell Betsey her son had come over late last night as well. I'd told him essentially I would keep his private business private and I intended to do just that.

"Dog's a good judge of character," Tambre said, coming up to the counter and placing three more of the pottery pieces. "That girl has been a bad seed for years." She was the opposite of Betsey as she didn't talk a lot. Her demeanor was cotton soft, which was rare for a Dragon Runner old lady, but somewhere in that gentle persona of hers was a hard core of steel. She might not say a lot but when she did, her words held weight. She was buying five pieces of pottery this time and the pottery wasn't cheap. She must really like it to get so much at one time. The artist would be thrilled.

Betsey put her soap on the counter as I wrapped the pottery up in protective bubble sheets. "You gonna come set up at the club's Halloween barbecue, ain'tcha? Got little over a month to finish plannin' it, but cain't hurt to start early."

I smiled and blinked at her. "I have a vendor table there every year. It's a great way to kick off the Christmas season and I really appreciate the opportunity. The Dragon Runners do so much for the community, I wish you got more recognition for it."

Betsey snorted. "Yeah, well, it would be nice, but that ain't gonna happen. Too many folks still remember how it was years ago before my Brick took over. Blue's dealing with this new drug mess in town now and the club is being eyeballed for it. Ain't no way! Fact of the matter is we want to catch the ones doing this shit just as bad as the sheriff does."

Tambre inhaled softly. "That's club business, Betsey."

The red-haired woman flipped her hand up and blew out. "Psssht! Ain't only club business when the town already knows there's somethin' goin' on."

She changed subjects and gestured at the building across the street. "Blue's living in one of them shithole apartments up there. Lord have mercy, I want him to move so bad. Jonelle got the court to declare he cain't have the kids overnight 'cause he's only got one bedroom. Don't matter, he'd sleep on the floor if he had too. She's also tryin' to get the court to say the kids cain't stay overnight up to the Lair anymore. Say it's not a 'safe environment' at a biker club." Betsey held up air quotes to match her sarcastic tone. "That ain't gonna happen. That woman spent time around the club when she and Blue were together and knows it's one of the safest places to be for a kid. The boys get rowdy and they do party, but not when kids are around. Now Blue's headin' back to court again, fighting just to keep what little time he gets. Damn that bitch! Blue won't take no money from Brick and me to help out. He's such a stubborn little shit sometimes!" she declared, looking at the ugly brick façade. Her tone softened. "I wish he would. He'd give up his last dime to take care of them kids. Don't have many men like that no more. My boy works hard and deserves to be treated right."

I wasn't sure why Betsey was laying it out to me, but I felt the older woman needed an ear. Sometimes people don't want answers, they just want someone to listen. I can do that.

Her voice broke a little and her eyes grew moist. "You know, he and his daddy had a little falling out over him wanting to be a law officer. Kinda goes against the grain for a Dragon Runner to be a deputy, don't it? Well, Blue didn't join up to spite his daddy. Brick has been the president and leader of the club for over thirty years now and he's not stepping down till he's drooling in a wheelchair or the good Lord takes him home. If Blue stayed in the club, he'd always be second to his daddy and that didn't sit too well with him. Blue's just like Brick, born to be a leader and protector. He's dancing to Jonelle's tune only because he has to for his kids' sake, but I know it's hard on him. Hard enough, I'm afraid he's gonna break."

This time a real tear flowed down Betsey's cheek. Blue wasn't the only one who was on the verge of breaking. My heart clenched at the sight. "Blue is a good man, Betsey, and one I'm grateful to have working for us in this town. I'll be glad to stand up for him in court if he needs me to say what I saw during the festival. He already knows that and if it helps him or the kids, I'd be honored."

Betsey dashed her red-tipped fingers under her eyes. "Thank you for helpin' him an' the kids out, Psalm. You're a good woman."

I nearly choked. I disguised the sound by ringing up Tambre's purchase and smiling at the total. "I think you just made this artist's day. Thank you so much for supporting him."

Tambre handed me her debit card and smiled back. "No problem. Local artists, local business. Keeps the money circulating in our own town instead of off in the internet somewhere else."

I loved these extraordinary women.

"If you want to donate some stuff, I'm holding a silent auction at the Halloween party to raise some money to help the families of them kids pay for the hospital bills," Betsey said, getting herself together.

"Or the funerals," Tambre added, reminding us that this

was a serious problem.

The ladies made their purchases and left. Betsey insisted I take her cell number in case the kids ever ended up in my shop again and I needed someone to come get them. I took it as it was easier than arguing with her.

CHAPTER 11

The next few weeks were fairly routine. Blue and I went through our morning ritual at the coffee shop and I made a point of smiling and blinking at him, telling him nonverbally that everything was fine in my world. If he made it to the coffee shop first, he would buy me a cup and have it waiting. If I arrived there first, I did the same for him, but he would frown at me for it, saying he should be the one to buy. We would chat about the weather, the high school football season, the town council, and whatever current event was taking place. He would help me with my shipping run. Then he would go to his work and I'd go to mine. Occasionally, he would text me at night when he saw my lights on late. He would ask if I was okay and how my day went. I would respond, telling him something positive that had happened. I even made up a few bits just to have something to say that was good. He still had the town to protect and so far there weren't any breaks in the drug overdose cases. I knew it was wearing on him and anything that could be uplifting would be good for him to hear.

Sam continued to blossom under my care and became more and more social. He started play-bowing a lot and trying to entice the other dogs to romp with him. They all played and wrestled together, even Toto, although she didn't participate in the festivities for very long. Sam did seem to gravitate toward kids and was especially pleased to see Cody and Michelle the few times their grandmother brought them to the store after school or when we ran into them at the playground area. Sam had his favorite rope toy that he would shake and play-growl at the little boy to take and throw. Cody would laugh like crazy when the hulking dog bounded after the toy and pounced on it. I didn't think either of them ever would tire of the game.

I saw Blue at the park sometimes too, usually still in uniform. He would sometimes talk to me if the kids were playing with the dogs and other times he would be playing with his kids on the equipment, not caring if anyone saw him monkeying around. I loved watching him chasing the squealing kids around, pretending to be a monster. Seeing Blue mess around with Cody and Michelle made me regret agreeing to Adam's decision. He didn't want to leave me alone to raise a kid by myself nor did he want to put that burden of losing a parent at a young age on a child. I admit, it would have made things harder, but I would have managed to make it work. I would have embraced motherhood and cherished every moment I was allowed the privilege.

It was early, but the evenings were getting darker and colder earlier. I still made the trudging walk to the park and stayed as long as I could every evening. The dogs needed the space as much as I did while we still had the weather and light to do so. There was a cold snap coming through and frost was in the air. I could see my breath forming steam as we walked the distance. I wore my heavy royal blue jacket and added a raspberry beret and mittens my Mom knitted for me. Even just walking to the park, I was going to be fashionable. The place was nearly deserted, but I could see Blue and his kids playing hard and staying warm. Cody let out a happy screech and ran toward Sam, who was carrying the shredding rope toy. He bowed and panted at the boy, dropping the slobbery knots at his feet. Sam seldom barked, but once in a while he would guff when he needed to make a point. Blue came over to where I was with a screaming and laughing Michelle hanging down by her feet over his shoulder. He righted her in a big swoop before setting her on her feet. She spun around dizzily for a bit before collapsing next to Toto and hugging the old dog.

"Hey, Psalm, how's it goin'?" he asked, his eyes full of happiness and a big easy smile on his face. This was as relaxed as I'd seen him in weeks. I knew why, too. The long-awaited court date was tomorrow morning and hopefully he would be settling the custody and visitation issues with his ex-wife. Holly was going to watch the store for me while I went to the courthouse in case I was needed. I hoped it would turn out well for everyone, most of all the kids.

"It's going well, Deputy. I hope your day was good and tomorrow is better," I said, hopping up to sit on one of the picnic tables.

"Today was good, in a way. Finally got a lead on the drug problem. Seems it's more localized to a few dealers rather than a pipeline. Homemade stuff in someone's basement somewhere, which is why it's so potent. Kinda like homebrew or moonshine. We think someone's been binge-watching *Breaking Bad* on Netflix. It's bled over to Dilsboro and clear up to Maggie Valley a bit. They've had some cases over in Cherokee as well on the reservation. All the sheriff departments in those counties are working with us to try and find out who's making the stuff. Got a couple of dealer names. Hopefully, we'll get 'em soon and trace it back to the source."

I smiled at him and turned my attention to the energetic children. Michelle and Cody both were pulling on the rope toy and Sam was dragging both of them.

"That is one damn strong dog," Blue remarked, taking a cigarette pack from his pocket and then putting it back. *No smoking around the kids*, I thought. Or else no smoking around me as per my dictate in my store. "I know you're just fostering him and so far everything is good, but I still think he's dangerous."

"Yes, he is a strong dog and your objection is duly noted," I replied, grinning, tucking my mitten-covered hands in my pockets.

"I want to thank you again for coming to the courthouse tomorrow morning. It really means a lot to me." He sat on the picnic table next to me.

I placed a hand on his shoulder and leaned on him a bit. I didn't think he would appreciate a full hug even though I thought he needed it. "It's no problem, Deputy."

"I'm off duty. You can call me Blue." He touched my hand still at his shoulder, and my stomach jumped. Such simple gestures were the ones I missed the most about being with someone, and I treasured every one of them.

We sat side by side in silence for a minute or two. It didn't feel awkward and we didn't need words between us. We just watched and listened to the kids and the dogs playing. Blue kept looking at his watch and scowling deeper and deeper. Jonelle was late. It was getting colder and the kids' enthusiasm for play dropped with the temperature.

A pair of headlights finally showed up, swinging across us as we sat side by side. The pickup truck was older and the kind that had two little jump seats in the back. Jonelle got out of the passenger side while the man with her stayed put, only the outline of his head and shoulders visible. She held on to the door as if trying to keep her balance.

"Michelle! Cody! Get over here, now!" she yelled.

"Fuck, no," Blue muttered as he got up from his perch on the table. The two children turned off like robots, but made no move to run to the car. All three moved slowly to the vehicle while I remained where I was. I figured Blue wouldn't appreciate an audience and the best I could do was to stay back. Gone was the jovial mood, killed like a mouse caught in a snap trap. Even the dogs were subdued—all except Sam. He stayed by my side but was watching the kids with laser focus, and his hackles were raised and rigid. He was silent, but I could feel his anger and fear as he stared at the truck and the people approaching it.

Heated words were exchanged, and even though I couldn't hear them very well, they were still loud enough for me to catch a few phrases. I could see Blue getting agitated. His back went ramrod straight at one point. Jonelle kept shaking her head and pointing her finger into his chest and yelling in his face.

"None of your fuckin' business!"

"I ain't that drunk! Billy's driving!"

"You cain't do shit 'bout it, neither!"

I was sure that he wouldn't let the kids go with her in that condition and was shocked when the two children climbed into the tiny back part of the cab and left. Blue held himself back, still as a marble statue until they pulled out of the parking lot. Then he exploded.

"Fuck!" he screamed at the top of his voice and hauled a fist back, punching at the wooden sign that held the park hours and information. The wooden planks splintered and flew in all directions from the force of his rage. I hurried over, Sam at my heels and the other dogs following.

"Blue! Are you hurt? What can I do?" I grabbed his hand to see what damage he had done to his knuckles. I wished the kids were there, as I bet they needed hugs and comfort as well. Tears formed in my eyes and I prayed that they were okay.

Blood dripped from Blue's knuckles and he was breathing fast and heavy as if he'd just run a marathon. His face was hard with barely contained fury and his eyes met mine with blasting anger.

"You're off the hook for tomorrow. I need to check

my e-mail to confirm, but according to Jonelle, court is continued. She got it moved back to the first of December. The judge is a distant cousin of hers by marriage. Just far enough away in the family tree to not be a conflict of interest and just close enough to make it work."

My mouth was hanging open a bit at this news and could almost taste the bitterness in his words. It still didn't tell me why he allowed his children to get in a car with a man he didn't know and a drunk woman. I wasn't familiar with all the legalities of custody, but surely he had some rights?

Don't judge, Psalm. He had to have a good reason, right? "You really let Michelle and Cody get in the truck and leave?" was what actually came out of my mouth. "Jonelle is drunk. Why did you do that?"

"Let it go, Psalm," he raged.

I knew his anger wasn't directed at me but I couldn't stop myself from prodding the bear.

"Let it go? You can't just order me to 'let it go'! I can't believe you just let your children get in a vehicle with those two!" I said, my own ire rising.

"You don't know everything, Psalm." Apparently, he wasn't going to share, stalking off to his patrol car and slammed his hands down on the hood.

"Get in and I'll take you and the dogs home," he snarled between clenched teeth.

I wasn't afraid, but for the first time I was mad. Furious at him for allowing the kids to be put into what I thought could be dangerous situation. I knew Jonelle had a temper and wouldn't be surprised at all if she took that temper out on the kids. How could he allow this to happen?

I loaded the dogs into the back and Toto up front on the floorboard at my feet. It was a tight fit but the distance wasn't very far and I fumed every second of the trip. He pulled his car into the spot in front of his building and walked the dogs and me across to my house. I unlocked the door, planning on stomping inside and not speaking, but I couldn't help it. The dogs rushed in the open door, eager to find their water bowls.

"What about a different judge? Can't you ask for one? You're a damn deputy in this town. That should count for something!"

"Psalm, let it go."

"No, I will not!" I exploded. "You're right, I don't know everything that's happening in your life and those children's lives, but what I see right now sucks and someone needs to figure out how to deal! What about one of those emergency hearings? I've heard they can be called at any time for any reason and I just saw plenty of them."

"Psalm, I'm telling you, stay out of it."

I supposed I should have got a clue from the cold voice coming from Blue's mouth, but I was on a roll and not ready to get off.

"Blue, this is wrong and you know it!" I emphasized that with a finger pointed at his face.

He responded by grabbing my offending digit and pulling me to his body. His mouth slammed down on mine, kissing me. It was hard and short but enough to stun me into silence. He stomped over to his building, and a minute later he was back out on his bike, roaring away down the street and leaving me standing on my porch alone. I looked at the dancing moths under the overhead light and raised a hand to my lips, still feeling the imprint of his. I was more confused than ever about this man, his complicated life, and what my role was supposed to be in it.

I went through my nighttime routine, feeding the dogs, cuddles and scratches, but none of us was in a good place. The dogs were downcast and restrained, climbing in bed with me as I tried to get to sleep. An hour later I was up again, looking at the dark windows across the street. I went down to my workroom, thinking about Cody and Michelle, full of worry about where they were and what was happening to them. I unmolded several long loaves of soap, but even the fresh linen and piney fragrances didn't help my mood. I was angry. Yes, me! Psalm Kopolove was angry. Angry for the suffering of those beautiful children. Angry for their asinine mother who was using them more as a tool for revenge than being a true parent to them. Angry their father was so freaking helpless. Angry there was nothing I could do about it. I set up the cutter and began slamming the sharp steel plate through the soft soap, but instead of admiring the colors and patterns I'd created, I imagined it was various body parts of Jonelle that I was cutting up. The cutter hit the board over and over. Thwack! There went the hand that rudely put a cigarette out on my work counter. Thwack! There went the one that pulled at Cody. Thwack! There went her snarky, jeering mouth. Thwack! Thwack! Thwack!

I'm not a violent person and would never consider getting in a fight with someone; however, I did feel better after slicing up the loaves I had made several days ago. I guess there was something cathartic about working out one's anger physically. I was glad I'd chosen to do it productively with my soaps instead of punching through a wooden sign. I lined the newly cut soap bars on the drying shelves and wrote the dates of production in the batch log. I was finally tired enough that I thought I could sleep. I had to move several dog bodies to make room, but I managed to secure my spot. I looked out at the still dark window and prayed again for the safety of the children and their father.

***

Blue pounded the bag, his already damaged hands throbbing in his boxing gloves. As a deputy, he had twenty-four-seven access to the station gym, and tonight he took advantage of it. No one else was around this time of night to watch him take out his anger on the swinging bag. He was sweating profusely, but his sour mood wasn't getting any better and he had the urge to go to the Lair or the Rivers Edge bar and get rip-roaring drunk. He quelled it as not many townspeople would be pleased to see that behavior from their deputy.

"Fucking bitch!" he muttered. No one was around to hear him, so he was able to let loose a bit. He was tired, bone deep tired of the bullshit he had to put up with from his ex-wife, but he still had to take it. Psalm had given him shit tonight about him rolling over for Jonelle to fuck him again, but what choice did he have? The pretty blonde shopkeeper didn't know everything.

He punched the bag hard enough to send it flying backward, and it nearly knocked him over on the return trip. He wished his biker friend Table was around to spar with, but that club brother was dealing with shit of his own.

Maybe Psalm was up and he could watch her work for a bit, even though he knew it was making him seem like a creeper. She was mad at him, but she was ever the optimist, which was something he needed, and even just observing her putter about her workspace, creating more stuff, was soothing for him. He had given in to his impulse to kiss her and the brief taste remained. He wished he could be with her more, take in more of her kindness and her calming influence, but right now he had to remember he had too much shit to deal with and wouldn't want to taint her with it. Still, he wanted her. He *really* wanted her.

CHAPTER 12

It was the sound I had been dreading for months. Hard gasping breaths, loud and unyielding, heralding another long and severe seizure. I took one look at Toto and knew this was it. She was as stiff as a board, her legs rigid as they spasmed in front of her prone body. Her eyes were fixed and dilated and she was panting hard, foaming at the mouth.

It had been less than a week since Blue and I spoke. I saw him at the coffee shop, but we'd been buying our cups separately, reduced to nods instead of words. Pam had been all smiles every time we'd come in the door and was now looking between us in puzzlement. I was still hurt and confused about what had happened at the playground and on my front porch. As many times as I'd told myself Blue had good reason to allow a drunken Jonelle and her scuzzy boyfriend to take the children, I still couldn't agree with him and there was an ache in my gut when I thought about what those two little ones were having to deal with.

Now my dog was dying.

My heart in my throat, I turned to Eva who had come to drop off some more lap quilts she had made. "Can you watch the store and the other dogs for me? Toto's really bad and she needs to get to the vet. This may take a while." I was glad my voice didn't waver. It wasn't time for me to break down just yet.

"No problem. Go do what you need to do and I hope she gets better," her eyes held both understanding and sympathy. Thank the Lord for other dog lovers, but this time Toto wasn't going to get better.

I covered Toto with her favorite plaid blanket and scooped her up. She was not a light dog and I staggered a little under her weight. She didn't move or react. The vet's office was a few blocks away, but I knew I couldn't carry her that far. I put her in the passenger seat of my truck and drove over there, crooning to her as she lay panting and huffing. I felt the tears hit my eyes and dashed them away. *Later, Psalm,* I told myself. *I can do this part later.*

Eva must have called ahead, as Dr. Jackson met me at the door with a gurney. I lifted Toto onto it and followed the rolling table into the clinic on the emergency side. She pushed the contraption past the other people in the waiting room. I didn't look to see who was there; my focus was on my dog.

Lindsey started an IV, took vitals as she always did, but I could tell this was only because of procedure. She knew as well as I did what the outcome of this visit would be.

"I'm giving her a relaxant to loosen her muscles and get her out of this spasm." Her brown eyes met mine, her face solemn. Her lips thinned as she pressed them together, her bright red lipstick disappearing. "You know what I'm going to say," she said, her voice quavering a bit. She had been Toto's vet ever since I moved back home with the tiny ball of fluff I had adopted so many years ago. This was affecting her as well.

I bit my own lip and nodded. "Yes, I think it's time."

She nodded back. "I'll leave you alone for a bit."

Toto's body had finally relaxed and her heavy labored panting had stopped, but she was still staring off into the distance, her big brown eyes dilated and confused. I stroked her thick brown and gray hair.

"Long time, eh, girl?" I said, the tears gathering. "You've been with me since it all started, back when my shop was nothing more than a dream. We've been through a lot, both good and bad. Lot of other dogs have come and gone through our house, but you were my first and always mine. Mine and Adam's. Love you, girl."

She pushed a paw to rest on top of my hand near her head. She could hear me and responded so I knew she was still with me. Her simple gesture, one she had done many times over the years, broke me. The tears started streaming down my face unchecked. I heard the door to the exam room open up and I turned, ready to deny what was coming. That I wasn't ready yet. Instead of Dr. Jackson's ample frame, Blue stood in the doorway wearing his khaki deputy uniform, one hand on the knob and the other grasping the doorjamb. I didn't say anything. He came over to me and laid his arm over my shoulder, holding me close to his side.

He reached out his other hand to stroke over Toto's coarse brown hair.

"Easy, girl," he murmured, to both me and my dog. "I went by the store and Eva told me what happened."

I knew he was still on duty but was glad he took the time to come be with me now. We just stood there, the two of us, stroking my dog, finding comfort in that simple, silent action.

I heard Dr. Jackson come back into the room and move off to the side. She would stay there all day until I gave her the go ahead. I brushed my eyes, looked over at her and nodded.

"Do you want to stay in the room?" she asked.

"Yes," I managed to say. My dog was not going to die alone. I was surprised how steady I felt. Blue's strong presence held me up.

The vet moved to where the IV was dripping into Toto's front paw and drew two full syringes from her pocket. This was not the first time I had witnessed this procedure, but it was the first time I watched it happen to my own pet. She pushed the needles one after the other into the IV tube and emptied the contents. About a minute later, Toto closed her staring eyes and breathed out a long breath as if sighing in relief that it was finally over.

I felt my heart. It was breaking. Physically, painfully breaking, but I still had to hold it together, just a little longer. Blue pressed me tighter against his body. I stifled my tears long enough to ask for Toto to be cremated, sign the necessary papers, and swipe my debit card to pay for everything. Dr. Jackson's eyes were suspiciously wet and I expected she too would be crying later.

Blue stayed right by my side while Lindsey wheeled Toto's body into the back room, where she would be transported to the facility they use for cremation. I would get a cherrywood box with her ashes in a few days.

Blue didn't let me go to my truck, but led me to his patrol car. I didn't protest when he took me back to my store and guided me in the door and up the stairs to the upper floor. I looked through the back hallway window that looked out to the courtyard where the other dogs were lounging in the sun. Blue stood behind me, holding me against his broad chest, wrapping me up with his strong arms across my middle. He didn't say anything. He didn't have to. He could feel the hurt coursing through my body.

Zeke was the first one to notice me and sat up, looking at me with his two different colored eyes, head cocked over and ears standing up. He whined once and then threw back his head in a long mournful howl. Dion curled up next to him and cried out himself. Sam was the only one who didn't make any noise but sat with the others, his head hanging low to the ground.

I'd held it together until then, but watching my dogs grieve our pack's loss was too much. I lost it.

Blue turned me and held me to his chest, letting my tears soak into his uniform. I wasn't a pretty crier. My face got blotchy, my eyes swelled, and my nose plugged up, making my voice sound funny. This was not my favorite look and I tried to avoid it when I could, but at the moment, all I could do was cling to the solid man who held me in an iron grip, stroking his hand up and down my back.

"Let it out, baby," he crooned at my temple. "You're allowed. Take all the time you need. I'm not going anywhere." He kissed my hair gently, giving me an anchor.

How could I stay mad at this man? If I wasn't so upset, my mind might have latched on to the fact that he just called me baby.

I didn't know how long my crying jag lasted. It could have been a few minutes, it could have been much longer, but eventually I emptied myself, leaving a huge wet spot on his khaki shirt. I didn't really want him to see the wreck that my face had become and didn't want to move either. He solved that dilemma by lifting my chin with his fingers and covering my mouth with his, softly but firmly kissing me.

***

Blue tasted the salt of her tears as she finally cried herself out. He knew Toto was her special dog, the one that had been with her the longest. Her grief was sharply acute and he felt how far it went. He stroked his tongue across her lips, asking for entrance. She made a noise and opened up to let him in. He rubbed her back more to soothe as he explored her mouth, licking at her lips, sucking the lower one and touching it with just the tip of his tongue. She burrowed closer, her breasts pressing against his chest. He could feel her need for comfort and it was something he was able to give. She was hurting and it was his job to take care of her, a role he gladly accepted.

He was still reluctant to leave her and forced himself to back off, end the kiss, and ease his grip around her. She hesitated before doing the same.

"I'm sorry for getting your shirt all wet." She sniffed and tried to discreetly wipe her streaming eyes before facing him. "I have Kleenex in my room." They moved down the hallway to her front bedroom. He leaned over and snagged a tissue box from her nightstand and handed it to her. She jerked three of the soft papers and pressed them to her face but only succeeded in smearing more mascara under her eyes.

"You're allowed to cry, sweetheart," he imparted. "She was a good dog and you gave her a good life."

Her watery gray eyes rose to his and he couldn't help it. He pulled her back in for another kiss, sweet and gentle, while pressing her tight against him and wrapping her body with his. He stroked his hands over her hair and back as he deepened the kiss into something more than comfort. Psalm was fast becoming more than just a friend he had coffee with on a daily basis. The thought thrilled him and terrified him at the same time.

A muffled guff broke through the haze surrounding his mind. He glanced to the side of the bed to a pair of curious gold eyes. Other pairs of canine eyes were watching as well, heads cocked to one side in curiosity. The dogs had come in through the doggie door at the back and were now surrounding him and Psalm. The faint tinkle of the front doorbell sounded in the distance and indistinct female voices drifted up from the shop floor. Blue closed his eyes as reality crashed back into his brain. Psalm was willing and needy in his arms and it would be easy to take what she was offering but it would be wrong on so many levels. He had nothing to offer back but heavy baggage. He was living on a shoestring budget, dealing with a bitch of an ex-wife, working nearly round the clock to investigate the sudden drug problem in town, and desperately trying to find time to be a father to his two children. It would be easy to forget his problems for a few minutes and lose himself in the possibility of a future with her, but that wouldn't respect her or her grief now. He reluctantly pulled back from her.

"Sorry for grabbing you, Psalm," he said roughly. "I didn't mean to come on so strong, especially now. It won't happen again. Forgive me?"

She took a shuddering breath, visibly rallied herself, and smiled through her tears. "Nothing to forgive, Blue. Everyone needs human contact from time to time. It was just a kiss. Toto was a good dog and I knew this time was coming. I'm okay with it as I know she had a good life and is now in a better place, somewhere across that rainbow bridge. Thank you for being here for me, but I know you're still on duty and have other stuff to do. You best be getting to it."

She moved back and brushed her hands over the front of his shirt as if wiping herself off him. He really didn't like that idea. He turned and began opening and closing the drawers in her bureau. "Where do you keep your pajamas?"

"Middle one on the left. I don't have pajamas, only nightgowns."

"Eva can cover the store today and if not, you can just close it. You get some rest and I'll text you later tonight," he ordered, shuffling through the drawer's contents and eventually pulling out a gown of cream-colored lace. He handed it to her. "Here, I'll step out while you get changed."

He stood in the hallway, shifting from foot to foot and trying not to imagine seeing her in the thin gown he handed to her. *What the hell am I doing?* he admonished himself. *She's hurting in there and all I can think about is kissing her again. Friends, Blue. You're supposed to be friends!*

The problem was he didn't want to be just friends. He wanted more. So much more. He didn't know when it happened, but he had fallen for this kind and gentle woman. It wasn't about lust for her gorgeous body, and it wasn't about a fling to get her out of his system. This was something that could be very real and it both thrilled him and scared him.

She can't know, he told himself. *She's too good for me and doesn't need to be in my shit storm life. I've got to keep it to myself and just be friends, even if it kills me.*

He tamped down his thoughts and buried them deep before tapping on the door and entering. Psalm was in the bed, the comforter up to her chin. The dogs had joined in and were curled up around her. He sat on the bed, his hip next to hers. Sam regarded him for a moment before grunting and rolling over.

"I see you'll have plenty of company for a while. No late-night crafting tonight. You need some real sleep."

She smiled again and dropped her eyes to the floor. "No

promises, but I'll do my best."

Blue had the urge to tip her chin up and take her mouth one more time but instead he pressed his lips to her forehead and reluctantly moved to the door. Outside, he took one last look at the second-floor window. His gut churned with the desire to go back up those steps and finish what he started, but with an iron will, he forced himself into his car and drove off, wishing like hell life would be different.

CHAPTER 13

The Dragon Runners' Halloween party was always held on the Saturday closest to the holiday at their campground pavilion. It was a huge affair with Betsey's barbecue, rides, craft vendors, games, costumes, the whole nine yards. What made the event even bigger was the collection for those kids and the families who were hurt by this drug epidemic. Since Main Street would pretty much be a ghost town today, I closed the store and set up a booth at the party with lots of soaps, shampoos, lotions, and other bits. I sold my own stuff at the craft fairs and my other artists had the option of working their own booths.

I'd been up since the butt crack of dawn, loading the tables, chair, canopy cover, and boxes of soap into the truck. The dogs were restless, but I couldn't take all of them. I wasn't planning on taking any dogs with me but decided at the last minute to include Sam. He was so good with kids and had never shown any aggression to anyone but Jonelle. I felt okay in bringing him also on the off chance

Cody and Michelle would be there and would enjoy seeing the dog. It was cold when I loaded the truck, so I wore a lined jacket in the morning, but by the time I got to the site, unloaded, and set up, I was sweating like crazy. The sun was up and although the day was slightly overcast, there wasn't supposed to be rain for a few days. Today would be cool and comfortable and, just to be cheeky, I wore a policewoman's costume complete with hat, plastic badge, foam baton, and plastic handcuffs. Instead of trousers, I wore black leggings and flat suede boots to finished my ensemble. I wasn't going to spend the next ten hours or so in heels! Blue had already made his patrol rounds and had rolled his eyes at my ensemble.

The booth stayed busy, people coming through the vendor area in droves. Eva's booth was set up next to mine, loaded with quilted jackets, lap quilts, scarves, handbags, and other bits she had sewn. She had just found out she was pregnant and was complaining of morning sickness. She was also showing off the ginormous rock on her left hand. Her old man, Stud, had finally popped the question and I was really happy for her.

Stud came by about midday and brought her some food. "How's my baby mama?" he asked, kissing her on the lips loud and long.

"I'm tired and I hafta pee again!" she grouched.

He laughed. "That's my cactus. Always a ray of sunshine!"

She grinned at him, unable to keep her bad mood.

He turned to me. "Hey, Psalm. You need anything?

We're getting ready start the Tail run in a bit for the kids. I can bring you some food if you need it."

"No, I brought stuff for me and Sam, but thanks so much for thinking of me."

"No problem, Psalm. You've been a real help to Eva and me, and the rest of the club. You ever need anything, we got your back."

He winked and kissed his future wife one more time before leaving to start giving kids short rides on the infamous road.

They have my back, eh? The Dragon Runners were such a great club and great family even if you weren't really a part of it.

People kept on coming to the vendors in long waves. So much so, I barely had time to wolf down the sandwich I brought. Eva and I spelled each other for quick bathroom breaks as we needed it, but there wasn't a lot of time for many of them. I left treats out for customers to give to Sam as they browsed my booth and had had to fill the bowl up three times already. I'd positioned my tables in a U shape under the canopy, leaving a small spot at the side for me to sit and Sam to lounge. He lay under the tables snoozing most of the time but would come greet people when they recognized him and called his name. Some people offered one of the doggie biscuits from the table and he would gulp it down. Sam was getting more and more social and comfortable with people in general. Soon it would be time for him to be put up for a forever home. My heart twinged a little at the thought.

My parents had set up a table close by and my dad was selling produce from his garden. He had several tables of different squashes, beans, and other vegetables, as well as a small mountain of orange pumpkins for baking or jack-o-lanterns. Mom was with him, of course, sitting in her fold-up camping chair and her hands busy with some new knitting project. I was always fascinated with the needles whipping in and out of the yarn too fast for me to follow and watching the stream of movement building a scarf or afghan. We waved and chatted for a bit, but the crowds kept everyone busy.

Later in the day, the throng finally thinned out. Eva had already packed up her booth and I was helping her load it in my truck to go back to the store when I saw Sam prick his stumpy ears forward and jump up, wagging the tiny knob that was left of his tail. His mouth opened up and his long pink tongue flopped out as he panted in a big doggie grin.

"Sam!" I heard a child's voice shout enthusiastically. A small figure in a stretchy black Batman costume and plastic mask came barreling up to the dog and threw his arms around the massive beast. Sam didn't bark but did whine a little and treated the child to a thorough face sniffing, nearly knocking the mask off. I laughed as the dog played, bowed in invitation, guffed at the boy in his deep doggie voice, and sniffed some more. Sam was clearly happy to see Cody and had recognized the boy before I did.

A pretty princess in a puffy pink tutu came up and was treated the same way with the face sniffing and doggie greeting. Michelle wasn't wearing a mask but sported a glittering silver crown.

"Well, I guess I know who you really wanted to see today!" I said, putting my hands on my hips and pretending to be offended.

"Oh! Hi, Psalm!" The miniature superhero piped up while Sam was enticing him to play with his well-chewed rope toy. The dog dropped the mass of strings at the boy's feet, bowed and barked at him to pick it up. Cody did and threw it as far as he could in front of the booth. Sam jumped and took off after the toy, scattering people around him in alarm. He pounced on it, shaking and growling at it as he brought it back to drop it at Cody's feet again for the next round. Michelle came and stood next to me.

"Daddy told me about your dog. I'm really sorry she died."

My heart bled a little. "Thank you, Michelle. That means a lot to me. That's a beautiful costume, but I'm not sure exactly what you're supposed to be. Are you a fairy princess or maybe a ballerina?"

The little girl said nothing, but shrugged and dropped to the ground to crawl under the table. The sounds of the crowd and the laughter of the little boy and dog playing faded away as I concentrated my focus on the girl sitting under my table. Not sitting. She was hiding.

I sat down myself and stretched my legs out, not caring if I got dirt or grass stains or even if someone came to my booth right then to buy something. This little girl took priority.

"Michelle, sweetheart? Are you okay?" I asked gently.

She sniffed and I saw a big tear roll down her cheek as she struggled not to cry out loud. She looked up at me with eyes so sad and hurt, I felt the need to cry with her.

"Come here, baby," I whispered and held out my arms. She crawled into my lap willingly and I held her close as she pressed her face against my shoulder and quietly sobbed. I could feel the tears gathering in my own eyes. I had no idea what was bothering the girl, but whatever it was, it was big.

I crooned and rocked her small body.

"I'll text Betsey to get Blue," Eva said, pulling out her phone.

"Don't bother, I'm here." I looked up into the Blue's tight face but didn't relinquish my hold on the crying little girl. In the background, I could see Sam playing a gentle tug-of-war with Cody. Blue was in full uniform and my girl parts appreciated his striking figure. I had to shake it off and remind myself that the child in my lap came first.

He squatted down and placed a hand over his little girl's head. "Babydoll, where's your mama?"

"Sh-she tol' me to st-stay at the rides 'n' watch Cody, but he ran off to come see S-Sam," she stuttered, trying not to lose it completely. "She g-gave me some money and tol' me t-to get corndogs and to stay a-away from Gramma's tent. She s-s-said she was g-going off wif Billy for a bit and would be back, but I-I ain't seen her in a long t-t-ime."

Blue was silent. I could see his jaw clenching, wishing he could explode but holding back for his kid's sake. Cody was still oblivious, but Sam was alert, standing a few feet away, holding the decimated toy in his jaws.

"I'm sorry, Daddy," the little girl whispered in a watery voice. "Please don't be mad."

That deflated Blue. "I'm not mad at you, baby girl. You did nothing wrong at all. Come here and give me one of your big daddy hugs."

Michelle crawled across my lap to get to him. She wound her arms tightly and fully around his neck and he held her small body as close as possible. Fresh sobs erupted from the child as she was held in a protective circle of her father's arms.

I couldn't help it. Seeing the pure love Blue had for his little girl, the total devotion he had to his children and his willingness to give everything he had was more than I could stand. I felt my own tears roll down my cheeks. I was falling for this man and these kids. He would never know it, but I would give everything for this beautiful family.

Blue took a few long minutes and let the girl cry on him, wetting his shoulder as she had mine. He finally looked up and spoke to me, his deep blue eyes abnormally bright.

"I'm still on duty till eleven. Mom's over at the pavilion dealing with the crowds and the Tail run. I don't know where Jonelle is and even if I did, I don't trust her condition. Would you help me?"

His voice was rough and broken. This was taking a bigger toll on him than I had imagined. What else could I do? I sniffled a bit and nodded. "Absolutely. They can stay with me at my place until you're off."

"Your daddy's almost done packing up. I'll get his keys an' take 'em over there now while you and your daddy pack up your stuff and get it loaded. Mos' folks done already gone over to the Tail party or home. No sense in staying any longer." My mom suddenly appeared, her familiar take-charge tone ringing overhead.

I got up from the ground. Mom always had a clear head in a crisis and I tried to do the same. "There's food in the fridge at the house. I expect the kids are hungry."

"S'long as you got meat, I got vegetables. I'll whip up somethin' for everyone. I'll keep back a plate for you, Deputy. Man's gotta have something warm at home after a day like today. Come on, little bit. Let's see what we can find over t' the house." She extended a hand toward Michelle, who took it willingly.

Cody had finally tired out from playing with Sam and wandered back to the four adults. Eva drove off to the Lair to find Stud and let him know what was happening. Her eyes were snapping fire and I knew she would have exploded by now in a fit of Irish temper had the kids not been around. The only hitch in the plan came when Sam insisted on staying with Cody. He jumped in the truck with the kids and wouldn't budge. Mom rolled her eyes at the stubborn animal but gave in and lifted Michelle into the cab. The truck was crowded, but no one minded.

Blue, my dad, and I finished loading the last of the soap bins into the bed of my truck. There weren't that many of them as I had sold out of much of the stock I had brought. It had been a good day for business, but not much else.

Blue loaded the last of the display tables and turned to shake my father's hand. "Thank you for everything, sir," he said firmly. "I can't tell you how much I appreciate your help tonight. I won't forget it. You ever need anything, count on me."

My dad took Blue's hand and pumped it twice. "Don't take bein' blood family to do the right thing, son. Everyone 'round here knows you're a good man and wouldn't blink twice to stand up for ya. Jus' keep takin' care o' them young'uns. The good Lord will see t' everythin' else."

He slammed the tailgate and turned to say one more sentence. "You wanna pay anyone back, then run for sheriff the next round. This town needs it."

Blue turned to me, his mouth silent but his eyes full of words. I hesitated but then reached out my hands out to him and he took both of them in his. I thought he really needed a hug but I wasn't sure how he would take it, so I settled for a good hand squeeze. Ever since Toto's passing, he had put more distance between us. Coffee and unloading my soap shipments in the morning was our only contact. He'd been polite but cold and less personal. I guessed he was regretting our kiss and backpedaling hard from it, maybe trying not to hurt me. Friends only, I had to remind myself. *Friends and nothing more,* my head said over and over again. Too bad my heart wasn't listening. I'd replayed the kiss over and over again in my head, the texture of his lips, the taste of his mouth, the thrill of his tongue playing with mine, and my heart wanted to burst. Yes, I was falling for this man so fast I was sure I was setting myself up for heartache, but the more I saw him, the more I thought he needed me. I just had to keep my feelings hidden, as he didn't seem to want or reciprocate those feelings. The few kisses we shared didn't really mean he cared about me. I may end up bleeding, but wasn't that what we did for people we loved?

"It's okay, Deputy. Do what you have to do. We've got your back. The kids will be fine until you get there," I stated firmly, hopefully hiding my real thoughts.

He looked at our joined fingers and frowned. "I'll see if Betsey can come get them, but she may not be able to for a while. If Jonelle shows up, call me immediately. Don't let her take the kids."

"I won't. I expect my mom is going to hang around for a bit. Please don't worry, Blue. I got this." I squeezed harder to make my point.

His tortured eyes lifted and met mine. He was breathing hard and I got the sense he was barely in control. I met his gaze with my own, steady and unyielding. He finally nodded and let go of me. I climbed into the cab of my truck and watched him stride off down the dark street to his squad car, his phone out and plastered to his ear. My dad had already fastened his seat belt and was waiting for me.

"That boy has a heap a demons t' fight. T'ain't right." He was full of country wisdom.

I agreed, but at the moment there were two small children that took precedent over anything else. We drove home talking about the day's sales, the upcoming cold snap, Thanksgiving plans at their church, anything but what was facing us at the house.

CHAPTER 14

The kitchen was warm and filled with the smell of some sort of stew and baking biscuits. My mom was a miracle worker in the kitchen and had run her church's Wednesday night suppers for years. Give her a half hour and she could put out a feast for thirty or more people. I still didn't know how she managed that feat, but I was grateful for it.

"I like to use more buttermilk in my biscuits, but she don't have none right now," my mom was saying. "This here will work till we get some."

Michelle was kneading more biscuit dough in a big ceramic mixing bowl, and Cody was carefully cutting out round biscuits with a floured drinking glass.

"Now careful not to work it too much. It won't rise up good. That's it! Good job, little bit," my mom coached while she kept her own hands busy. The simple praise had the little girl beaming as she flattened the dough so her brother could punch out more biscuits. My mom shifted over to take a cookie sheet out of the oven and the fragrance of fresh buttery bread filled the room. I inhaled the aroma in appreciation.

"What's fer supper, old woman?" my father bellowed as he entered the kitchen.

"A knuckle sammich iffen you call me old woman again!" she bellowed back.

Michelle giggled. I was filled with joy hearing it and laughed out loud myself.

"I put on cheeseburger stew. It's fast and fillin'. Psalm, stir in some flour to thicken it a bit. Cody, finish up them biscuits and go wash your hands. You too, sweetpea. Got more flour on you than in the bread pan. Papa, you get bowls and plates out th' pantry."

My mom was in military mode and I saluted her smartly, earning more giggles from the kids. They rushed to the kitchen sink and my dad stopped his task to lift them both in turn to reach the running water. I stirred the concoction in the big stew pot simmering on the stove, dipping out a bowlful of broth and mixing in a handful of flour before pouring it back into the stew. I turned up the gas to let the mixture boil and thicken. Small pieces of potatoes, carrots, celery, ground beef, and lots of cheddar cheese made up the stew.

In no time at all we were seated around the round table I had in the corner of my kitchen, my mom ladling out big bowls of the delicious stew and my dad handing out golden biscuits. He said grace and the kids dug in like they were starving. Michelle peppered the table with questions while we ignored Cody feeding little bits of bread to the dogs.

"Why did you cut the potatoes and carrot so little?"

"Makes 'em cook faster."

"Why's buttermilk better for biscuits?"

"Gives 'em more flavor."

"What makes them rise?"

"Bakin' powder 'n' eggs."

The questions continued as well as the patient answers. I wasn't sure who enjoyed it more, my mom or Michelle.

After everyone ate their fill, the kids cleared the table and my father started washing up. Neither one of my parents used the dishwasher, preferring to do everything by hand. The kids were fascinated and entertained by their bickering.

"You missed a spot, old woman."

"I ain't missed nothing."

"'S right here."

"That ain't no spot, that's a little chip out the side."

"You need new spectacles, old woman. That ain't no chip, it's a spot!"

"I'm fixin' to spot somethin' else, old man!"

The whole time they grumbled at each other, my dad was making faces behind my mom's back, and the kids were loving it with suppressed giggles and outright laughter. I started thinking this may be the first time, outside of Betsey and Brick, that they saw two married people tease and play with each other in fun, not in anger. The devotion my parents had to each other was obvious in their motions, if not their words. There was no doubt they were deeply in lasting love and would go to the mat if necessary to protect each other. I hoped with all my heart this was a teaching moment for the kids and they would carry this memory of tonight rather than what happened earlier today.

"I need to feed the dogs, although they're probably so full of bread by now they don't need dog food," I said, giving Cody a side glance, telling him I saw him biscuit sneaking. He grinned and shrugged his tiny shoulders.

Both kids scrambled to help me fill and put out bowls.

"How come you got so many dogs?" Michelle started in on me as we placed the bowls in front of the snuffling, wagging animals.

"Well, I started with just Toto. She was part of a stray litter of puppies that were found on the street. Their mama wasn't around so when the rescue agency had them ready to go, I took her in and had her until she passed. After that, I found another dog who needed a good home. And then another and another and before you know it, I had a houseful of dogs. I don't keep them all, but I take care of them until a forever home is found."

"What's a forever home?"

I smiled. "I'm what's called a foster mom for dogs. That means I give them a home until a family or someone else wants to give them a home forever. Sometimes I get dogs who've been hurt or not taken care of very well. My job is to love them, take care of them, and help them heal so they can go to forever homes and be happy."

Michelle's face turned shuttered and thoughtful.

"Does that happen with kids when their mama's not around?" she asked in a voice far too old for her.

I hesitated for a moment. This was getting into some

heavy stuff for a six-year-old mind and I needed to think about my answers and choose my words carefully. "Sometimes it happens with kids when the parents can't take care of them the way they should. It's never ever the kids' fault and sometimes it's not really the parents' fault either. Sometimes the parents don't have enough money or can't get a good job, or maybe have too much to do. When that happens, the kids can go to foster parents who do have money or good jobs and have lots of time for them. There are lots of reasons kids go live with foster parents for a bit, but let me tell you again, it's never in a million years the kids' fault."

"Mama was sick for a while and went away to a special hospital. That's what Daddy said. Me and Cody stayed with Gramma a lot when Daddy was working so Mama could get better. Mama's been mad since she got home and I think it's 'cause Daddy made her go away. Then Mama made Daddy go away and live somewhere else so we don't see him like we did. Mama said she'd dump us in foster care before she'd let Daddy have us again. What if she gets sick and has to go back to the special hospital?"

My heart jumped as a combination of anger and sympathy passed through me. This was worse than I'd thought. I could have gladly slapped Jonelle at that moment for ever saying that around these children. They were kids and supposed to be laughing and playing on the playground with dogs, not thinking about and dealing with life like miniature adults. I took the girl's hands in mine much as I had her father's a few hours ago and looked at her steady in the eye.

"Listen to me good, sweetheart. Are you paying attention?"

"Yes." Her answer was short and her voice uncertain.

"If your mother gets sick again, there is no way on this earth that you and Cody would go into a foster home. Your daddy would never ever in a million years let that happen. You have too many people in your family who love you and Cody to pieces to ever let you live with strangers. Your grandparents, my parents, me, and especially your daddy."

"Does Mama love us too?" she whispered.

My own throat clenched at the tiny break in her tone. "I'm sure your mother loves you. She wants you to stay with her more than you stay with your daddy and that's why they fight so much."

"I don't think that's why they fight. She's not around that much and we stay at Billy's watching TV most of the time while they're out."

I was seriously in over my head. How could I answer positively when all I felt was negative toward Jonelle?

"I'm still sure your mama loves you, sweetheart. She just shows it different."

Michelle's eyes still held doubts, but a familiar bellow came from the back porch.

"Supper's over and the cow's done been put up. Time for bed," my mother yelled, bringing up old memories of my own childhood. "I reckon them kids need some shut-eye after all the ruckus. Papa's done skedaddled back up the road t' the house. Imma stayin' the night. Y'all get in here and get washed up."

I leaned down to Michelle and whispered loudly so my mother could hear, "I think my mom was in the army when she was younger. She sounds like General George, doesn't she?"

"I heard that!" was the muted response.

Michelle grinned and nodded. I wasn't sure if she got the cartoon reference, but for now at least she was out of that heavy place in her head.

I texted Blue to tell him I was putting the kids to bed and to text me when he could.

Twenty minutes later, the kids were snuggled in my big bed, wearing my T-shirts to sleep in and delighted to be surrounded by canine bodies. They giggled at the dogs' antics of circling and pushing at each other to find the right spot, but didn't take long for them to conk out for the night. My mom was curled up in one of the guest bedrooms I had set up and was nose deep in an e-reader, the only modern piece of technology she was willing to touch because she could make the font big enough to see.

I settled on the couch in the sitting room next to my bedroom. Sam left the sleeping Cody and came over to join me for bit. "Good boy," I crooned softly as he pushed into my side. I scratched his ears and neck and he groaned, pushing my hand to the spots where he wanted the attention. "Rough night, eh? You were a big help to those kids, big guy."

I kept crooning and talking to him for a bit, just enjoying the private time, when my phone beeped a message.

Blue: On the way. Kids still up?

Me: No, they are out like lights, sleeping with the dogs. All of them are fit tight like puzzle pieces in my bed but it works.

There was a long pause and I thought for a minute he was done for the night.

Blue: I'm outside. Can I come in?

Sam grunted when I stood up and went back to climb on the bed with the kids and other dogs. Cody mumbled in his sleep and turned over, flopping one arm over Sam's big back. He didn't move. I crept down the steps, noticing my mother's light was off. She typically was in bed for the night long before this hour and was known to sleep like a rock. Blue was standing outside the back door. I could see his broad silhouette through the filmy white curtains. His handsome face was as long and tired as I'd ever seen it. Bags hung under his fatigue-glazed eyes and I was sure he was ready to drop.

"How are they?" he asked, his voice low.

I smiled at him. Of course, his first words were about the kids. "They're fine. Upstairs right now in my bedroom surrounded by furry bodies. You can take a look if you want, but careful of the third and fourth steps. They squeak pretty bad and you might wake them up."

He stepped lightly and slowly as we made our way to the upper floor. I had a brain flash to the last time he was here. He had been the first man in my bedroom since my husband. Warmth buzzed through me at the thought, but I knew this was neither the time nor really the place, as there were kids and dogs in there at the moment.

Cody lay on his side against Sam's back, one arm still flung over the dog's body. Sam cracked open an eye when we looked in but just grunted and settled himself again. Michelle was on the other side, corralled by Zeke. Dion was flopped at the foot of the bed. I smiled at the sight. What could be better or safer than to be surrounded by a pack of loyal canine guardians?

I leaned over and whispered, "You can't get more secure than that."

Blue didn't say anything, just turned the old-fashioned diamond glass knob and closed the door as quietly as he could. He motioned to go back downstairs.

"Are you okay with them staying here? I can wake them up and take them to my place if that's better for you," he whispered low.

I shook my head. "No need. They're fine where they are. I think the dogs are enjoying having them as well. You're welcome to stay here and be with them in the morning. I have plenty of rooms and the beds are already made up."

He looked like he wanted to take me up on the offer but sighed and closed his eyes, pinching across them with his thumb and index fingers.

"I can't. It wouldn't look right, even though your mother is here. I can't take any chances on the next court hearing. I found Jonelle at the beer tent with her boyfriend. She'd been drinking and got into a fight with someone. They're both at the jail drying out now. It's gonna be real cute tomorrow when my kids find out their daddy arrested their mama again. There's no way she'll keep that to herself and not take the first opportunity she can to share it with the kids. Fuck! I'm so tired of this bullshit!"

I felt the pain coming from him in waves. I hated that I had to add to it, but I had to tell him about Michelle's line of questioning. He leaned back and looked at the ceiling.

"Fuck," he repeated in a whisper, and closed his eyes. I could see wetness forming at the corners. "My little girl," he breathed. "That's my little girl."

How in all that is holy can this man deal with what life is handing him? "It's not your fault or your problem what Jonelle does. She's a big girl and can make her own decisions. She also has to accept the consequences of those decisions and that's not your problem. I'm sure this latest gambit of hers will backfire and, at the court hearing, you'll get your kids back. I'll be glad to help in any way and I'm sure my parents will as well."

Blue looked at me, his eyes unfocused and strange, and opened his arms wide in invitation.

I smiled and stepped into them.

* * *

Blue was at his breaking point. His life was such a roller coaster of emotions he felt he was losing his mind. His reality had become one of constant out-of-control chaos. The leads for the drug line had either come up empty or were being hidden by the club as they closed ranks, wanting to mete out their own form of justice. The sheriff was turning a blind eye to the happenings in town, which made the investigation even harder. He suspected his ex-wife was using again and he prayed she wouldn't become another overdose victim and put his kids through that hell. He didn't trust this new boyfriend of hers and the kids were getting more and more closed off every time he saw them. And now this mess. If something didn't get resolved soon, he thought he would snap and find himself looking at the bottom of a bottle to escape.

Psalm was the only constant calm in his life. She was the eye in the storm, the cool serenity that helped keep him sane. Her quiet words of support helped him keep the composure he needed so desperately to fight for his kids and his life.

He needed her more than he ever thought he would need anyone, and as selfish as he thought it seemed, he was going to take as much as she had to offer.

She wrapped her arms around him and pressed her full body to him, laying her head at his shoulder just under his neck. He nearly groaned and drew his own arms around her back and shoulders, pulling her closer. Her quiet strength was undoing him. The unconditional support, the comfort of her touch, it was almost more than he could take. His eyes closed as he put his nose to her hair and drew in the scent of jasmine.

"My door is always open for you," she whispered softly. He could feel her breath against his skin.

If she had stopped touching him then, if she had let him go, he might have been able to walk away. Instead, she leaned up and pressed her lips to his jaw, just below his ear. It was nothing more than a quick friendly peck, but it was the straw that broke the camel's back.

He broke.

His mouth slammed down on hers. She hesitated for a brief moment before opening her mouth and he dove in, their tongues tangling. Her taste was intoxicating, clean, sweet. He lost his fingers in her hair, moved her head to a better angle, and deepened the kiss. He needed this and took more and more. She didn't protest or pull away. She gave as he demanded, meeting his mouth and tongue with her own, her arms still around him, holding on.

He wrapped an arm around her lower back and pressed her body to his, feeling the softness of her breasts crushing into his chest. His hands lowered to her ass and he grasped a firm cheek in either hand, lifted her to the counter and spread her thighs to maneuver between them. She opened them wide and cradled his hips, hooking one leg behind him. He pushed his hardness into the well of her thighs, seeking her warmth and her wetness. His dick was up, hard and wanting more, aching for it. He could feel her wanting to give it. He could feel her....

He ripped his mouth from hers and jerked away. He spun around and planted two fists on the work table, his arms rigid as he fought for control. He wanted to bury himself in her soft, willing body so much he could taste his own need. Too much shit in his life, too much to focus on and fix for him to start something he wasn't sure he could finish. His heart was torn in so many places, he wasn't sure it was fixable and it was not fair to Psalm to use her and not give her more. She was not that kind of woman. She was the kind of woman you came home to on a nightly basis for dinner, talked about your workday, shared burdens, worshipped her body every night and thanked God every day that she was yours. He'd tried having that once and now his life was in complete turmoil. He wasn't sure he could ever find it in him to go down that road again.

He really wanted it to happen again. Over and over and over. So much so he didn't trust himself to turn and look in her direction, afraid if he saw her still sitting on the counter, legs open to him, lips swollen and red from his mouth, he would forget his resolve and spend the night buried inside her softness.

He growled and slammed his fist on the counter one last time before stomping out of the back door. "Lock this behind me," he snapped. Four minutes later, he was on his bike, roaring out of town to the bluffs, desperately seeking the peace he knew he would never find.

He reached his spot on the bluffs, turned off the bike, and stood watching the town lights twinkle. The holidays were coming, which meant more tourists for the railroad, and already Christmas decorations were up. The quaint little town would be a picture-perfect Norman Rockwell painting, yet Blue couldn't help thinking what a lie that was. Underneath the façade was a cesspool of lies, cheating, and drug abuse. He was still fighting, but he was so tired and the weight of his responsibilities was crushing him. He fumbled in his pocket looking for a cigarette and cursed when he didn't find one. He looked down at the Bowers house where his children were sleeping safe, at least for now, and Psalm, the woman he wanted so much but couldn't have.

Why not? I love her.

He pushed out the thought almost the second he had it, but it still burrowed like a worm into his brain. There was no peace up here on the bluffs tonight. He mounted his bike, deciding to head to the gym. Perhaps a few hours of heavy lifting and punching the bag would help. His phone chirped a text before he started the engine. He sighed and swiped open the screen on the annoying device only to raise his eyebrows at the message. For the first time, he saw a glimmer of hope.

CHAPTER 15

Blue didn't pick up the kids the next morning. Betsey did, stating Blue was busy at the jailhouse dealing with Jonelle's bail. Apparently, her parents had shown up and fronted the money to get her and her boyfriend Billy out of jail. The kids would have to go back to her unless there was a forced emergency hearing for custody. That wasn't going to happen on a Sunday afternoon. Betsey's eyes were red and swollen from her own weeping, but she put on a cheery face for the kids as she loaded them in the car. Cody talked about Sam and how smart he was. Michelle talked about biscuits and how you were supposed to make them with buttermilk. The only glitch was when Betsey tried to leave, Cody threw a huge tantrum about leaving Sam. Betsey ended up taking the dog with her just to keep the peace.

"I got an empty dog run in the backyard. Doghouse in there is old, but it's still in good shape. It'll do for a night or two. Cody, you can see Sam from your window?"

Cody didn't like the idea of Sam being outside, but

Betsey was firm about not having a dog in her house. I wasn't thrilled about it, but he would be sheltered and close to his favorite little boy, and that took precedence at the moment.

My mom had been up since the crack of dawn and was keeping herself busy in the kitchen cleaning out my refrigerator and complaining about the expired food. I just sat and ached. My head ached, my gut ached, and my heart ached. I texted Blue to let him know the kids were picked up and heading to the Lair with their grandmother. He didn't text back.

Today was Sunday, my official day off, and I packed up the dogs and my mom to get her back home and tried to get back to my routine. I was on a roller coaster of emotions and getting out of town was one way I could get myself settled. Or at least I thought so. I spent the day at my parents' house, puttering with my mom in the kitchen, helping her with canning up the last of the pole beans and winter squash from the garden. She could tell my heart wasn't in it but didn't say anything to me.

The ride home was somber and the dogs were whiney. Buddy was set to go to a new home in a few days and I was not particularly ready to let him go just yet. Zeke was wheezing a lot and I expected he was getting a doggie cold. My house felt empty and dead for the first time since I bought it. The windows in Blue's apartment across the street were still dark, as they had been all night last night.

I didn't really feel like going through my pamper night, but I forced myself to do it. I had a new hair mask recipe I wanted to try, one that could be made to market instead of just make-as-you-go. I was in my workroom area wearing my fluffy bathrobe mixing the ingredients when a knock on my door made me jump. I looked up, already knowing who I would see. There was only one person in the world who would knock on my door at this hour of the night. Blue spotted me through the filmy curtains of my back door window. His eyes opened in complete shock and he burst out laughing so hard I almost didn't let him in. I wished I could've scowled at him, but the clay mask on my face had already hardened some and would start cracking. My hair at least didn't have the oil mess in it yet and was up in a towel wrap on top of my head.

"Holy fuck!" he hooted as I opened the door, doubling over to catch his breath. "You look like a B-rated movie monster. What the hell is that stuff?"

"Face mud mask every Sunday," I said with as much brute force as I could. The hard mask was immobile and any movement pulled at my face. "Helps to tighten skin and prevent wrinkles." I had spent the last twenty-four hours going over and over in my head about Blue Davis blowing hot and cold. One minute kissing me like he couldn't let me go, and the next minute he shoved me away like a pariah. I was getting sick of it, but I still couldn't find it in me to abandon him.

He guffawed again. "If I had to put that mess on my face, I may just take the wrinkles." He went off into more peals and this time my face split with his mirth, the clay cracking open and flaking off.

"It's not that funny," I complained, losing my battle not to smile. "Now it's ruined!"

"Yes, it is, baby. Believe me, it's fucking hilarious!" He wiped at his eyes and stood up straight, still chuckling at my appearance. "Oh, Jesus H. Christ, I needed that."

I rolled my eyes but was secretly thrilled to see his merriment. If I could get him to smile like that by wearing a clay facial mask, I'd put one on every day.

"How much longer you gotta wear that shit?" he gasped out.

I sniffed, not quite ready to completely let go of my ire. "Since it's cracked now, I can rinse it off anytime."

"Well go do that, baby, and get some warm clothes on. We're going for a ride."

I blinked at the one-eighty degree turn of the man in front of me. I could get whiplash, as many times as he'd flipped. "We're what?"

He stopped all his gleeful noise and gazed seriously into my eyes. Something was different. "I'm taking you for a ride tonight. Go get changed."

I studied him for a moment. He was ordering again, not asking, which bugged the snot out of me sometimes. The bathtub was full and ready, my eBook reader next to it. My pamper night was calling my name.

"Give me ten minutes," I said, moving to the stairs. It took me just five before I was back downstairs, hair down, face cleaned off, dressed in jeans, a sweatshirt, and tennis shoes. He handed me my jacket and mittens before leading me outside to his bike and putting a full-face helmet on my head, fastening the buckle under my chin. He put on his own helmet and mounted the massive bike, kicking up the stand and motioning me to get behind him. I had never been on one before but had watched club women make this maneuver and thought I did well for a beginner. I clasped his waist in my hands, but he grabbed them and pulled me closer, snuggling me up against his warm back and thighs. He placed my hands across his hard stomach and I felt his muscles move as he started the bike and shifted it into the street.

"Hang on, baby," he said before we took off. The cold wind cut through my jeans and worked its way beneath the collar of my jacket. I shivered against Blue's back and laid my head on his shoulder to keep from clacking my helmet against his. Despite the extreme discomfort, I felt exhilarated. The movement of man and machine was flawless and his command of the beast had me twitching in my seat, suppressing the urge to grind against him. I groaned out loud, thinking he couldn't really hear me, but apparently he could as he moved his leather-gloved hand to cover mine as they gripped him tight.

We were traveling up a short mountain road, gliding through switchbacks several times before we left the pavement and started driving slower on a narrow gravel pathway. I knew we were on the bluffs, but I hadn't been through this particular part. He stopped at a wider area and cut off the bike's engine. He motioned for me to get off and he kicked down the stand for the bike, propping it gently. The air was cooler and quieter here. Not many insects twittered this time of year. It was as if the mountain was preparing for its winter sleep.

Blue took my helmet and I missed its heat on my head. He grabbed my hand and walked us closer to the edge of the bluff. We could see the whole town, its few street lights shining in the dark night. Off in the distance, on the top of another bluff, I spotted a bunch of lights indicating a large building. The famed Dragon Runners Lair. I shivered as the cold bit into me. My parents would say I'd grown soft, being as at this time of night I was usually ensconced in my second tub of hot water. Blue came up behind me and put his arms around me, enfolding me in his large warm body and leather jacket. I curled up and reveled in the heat.

I stayed silent, waiting for him to tell me why he'd brought me here. Why was he suddenly being so attentive? The line between friends and something more had been blurred more than once and I'd sworn that I would accept whatever he had to say and deal with any hurt privately. I let go of any residual anger I had at him. First and foremost, I would be his friend, and if that was all this was, then I would handle it, even if I lost a little piece of my heart as a result. Having him in my life in any capacity was worth it to me.

He buried his cold nose against my neck and I yelped and jumped.

"You always smell good. Like sunshine," he commented, ignoring my surprise.

I laid my arms on top of his as they held me around my waist. He fit me closer to him and I could feel his hard body pressing against my back. I shivered in the cold. "Is there a reason you really wanted to come up here tonight instead of staying in a nice warm house?" I could feel the tension getting denser in the air and began stroking my hands over his thick forearms.

"I come here often, as it's my private spot to think and sort things out in my head. I can see the whole town from here. It reminds me of who I am and why I do what I do. Sometimes I need that reminder."

He paused and I felt him press his lips against the point behind my ear. He spoke against my neck, his warm breath sending a different kind of shiver down my spine. "I needed to talk to you and tell you some pretty heavy stuff. This was the first place I thought of. Never brought anyone here before. You're the first person I've ever shared this spot with. Not Jonelle. Not even with the kids. I know it's cold up here this time of year, but this is where I get my head clearest. Make sense?"

I nodded, still feeling the thrill running through my body. Those pesky butterflies were back, flittering through my stomach.

Then he began speaking. And me? I stood with his cold nose against my neck and listened.

"I got a text from Molly when she was sitting duty last night at the office. Jonelle is fucked. This last stunt cost her the kids. Too many witnesses for her judge cousin by marriage to get her out of it this time. The lab tech is a friend of mine and rushed the bloodwork. Her tests came back positive for this new drug that's been floating around town.

I got an emergency custody order granted to me last night and a crisis hearing set for tomorrow morning. I think it's going to stick. It's not over yet, but there's a light at the end of the tunnel and I don't think it's a train this time."

This was good news in a way, but there were still two kids caught up in the cross fire between their warring parents. That war was ugly and could get uglier, but at least now there was a chance for a resolution and the children would hopefully come out on top. Whatever happened, I was planning on being there for all of them. "I'm happy for you, Blue. I'm sorry you and the kids still have a rough road ahead, but I'm glad things will get better for you."

"I have something else to tell you," he said, taking a deep breath. "I know you were mad at me for letting Jonelle take the kids when you thought she shouldn't and you were right. She's been walking all over me for years now and it's been hard to take, but I've let her do it over and over again. The thing is— Ah, Christ, this is harder than I thought." He paused, trying to find the right words.

I waited patiently, giving him time and courage to say what he needed to say.

He finally blurted, "Cody isn't mine."

If he hadn't been holding me, I might have fallen from shock. Of all the things he could've said, that was the last thing I expected.

"My name is on his birth certificate. I held him as a newborn, changed his diapers, took him to the doctor when he got sick, put clothes on his back and food in his belly. I love that boy with all my heart, just like I do Michelle. He is my son, just not of my blood. The laws are shaky when it comes to this kind of thing and Jonelle has held that over my head for the last year, threatening a DNA test to take him away from me and split the children up. I couldn't let that happen and I'll move heaven and earth to keep my kids safe. Both of them."

***

Blue breathed in deep the warm scent floating from Psalm's clean skin. He had originally gone to her house to apologize again and reestablish their relationship as friends and friends only. One look at the pink terrycloth tower balanced on her head and the gray mess on her face dispelled that completely. This was for him. The first of the day, he spent dealing with Jonelle's bail and her parents getting her out of holding. The rest of the day he worked on getting an emergency custody hearing set for Monday morning. He managed to push through and get a different judge than Jonelle's distant relative, citing the familial connection and conflict of interest. The court didn't flinch this time.

The new judge was a young idealist and out to prove herself capable of running with the big dogs in the county. Jonelle screwed up royally when she abandoned the kids in favor of the beer tent and then picked a fight with a woman she thought was flirting with Billy. She was spitting mad when he was forced to put her in cuffs and her pupils had been dilated and wild. The drug test proved she was using again and if it weren't in such bad taste, he would have danced a big ol' happy dance. This was the break he needed. The first person he thought of to share this news with was Psalm, but she had been out all day at her folks' place and he needed to spend time with Michelle and Cody, explaining what was happening to them.

He was amazed how they reacted to the news their mother had been arrested and there was a good chance they would be living with him from now on. Michelle cried a bit and hugged him, happier than he thought she would be about the move. Cody stuck his finger in his nose and asked if he could have a puppy. Right now, they were still up at the Lair getting spoiled by their grandmother. He spent the rest of the evening scouting new places to live since the massive amount of child support would presumably be reduced or stopped altogether. Spousal support would be stopped as well. Her distant cousin judge had granted it even though Jonelle was not disabled and could find a job. Blue expected the court to rescind that order and make her stand on her own two feet for a change. He was almost giddy with relief.

Psalm was here in his arms. He needed to clear the air with her. He was tired of fighting the attraction and there was no reason for him to hold back, so why should he? There was just one more bit in his life he needed to share, but if Psalm was the kind of person he thought she was, there wouldn't be any problem. He was ready for this. He still didn't know if he had a future with her or could commit to one, but at least for tonight, she was his. He hoped.

When he shared his news about Cody's parentage she was quiet. She had been caressing his arms absently while he talked and then stopped when he declared the love he had for his son, for both of his children.

The stillness was troubling.

"Psalm?" he breathed.

She answered by turning in his arms, putting her mittened hands on his cheeks and drawing his face to hers. One touch of her soft lips was all it took.

He devoured her mouth, his tongue tasting, licking, and sucking at her full lips. One hand went to the back of her head, angling it to the exact place he needed it to be. She held nothing back, letting him touch her, giving him everything.

His dick was hard and he expected the ride back to town would be rough. He pulled back, just enough to break away and breathe, but his mouth stayed close enough that his lips brushed hers when he spoke again.

"I can't tell what's going to happen tomorrow, next week, or anytime in the future. I sure as hell don't want to make promises I can't keep, but I know I need you now. I need your forgiveness for my anger and my stubbornness. I need your kindness and understanding for me and my children. Most of all, I need you to hold me tonight like you love me. Allow me that privilege."

It wasn't a question. It was a statement, but she nodded just a touch. Enough that made his body harden even more in anticipation.

CHAPTER 16

The ride back to town seemed shorter, perhaps because all he could concentrate on was the small female body behind him that would soon be under him.

He managed to control himself when they got into her house and up the stairs to her bedroom. The dogs seemed to sense they needed privacy and they left the room. He was glad he wouldn't have to toss them out.

Her room was very feminine without being overly frilly. The kids were safe at their grandmother's. He was off duty for a change. They had all night and there was no need to rush. He smiled at her as he pulled three foil packets out of his wallet and placed them on the nightstand.

"Pretty sure of yourself, aren't you?" she asked on a breathy laugh.

He smiled again and reached for her, taking her shoulders in his hands and drawing her close. "Yeah, baby, I am. I just hope three is enough." He sighed into her hair.

She bit her lower lip. "Um… it's been a very long time

for me, Blue. I'm a little… well, nervous I guess."

He kissed her again, long and slow. Taking the time to build the want. She clutched at his arms, whimpering into his mouth as she matched his tongue's movements with hers.

"I know, sweetheart. I live across from you and I've watched your place from the bluffs. The only males that have been in the house in years are your dogs. We'll go as slow as you need to. Trust me, baby, I got you."

His hands moved to the sweatshirt she wore and lifted the edge. She loosened her iron grip on him and raised her arms, giving him an unspoken answer. He stripped the shirt from her in one movement and dropped it to the floor. She hadn't bothered to put on a bra earlier and her pink-tipped breasts gleamed in the low light, her nipples tight. He filled one hand and lowered his head to take the stiff peak in his mouth, teasing and sucking it gently. Her head fell back and she moaned, arching her back for more. He raised her other breast, treating it to the same. Her arms lay around his shoulders as he played with her. He let her go long enough to pop the button on her jeans and push them down along with her simple cotton panties. He could feel her trembling as she stepped out of the garments, leaving her totally exposed to him. Her fingers fumbled at the zipper of his jacket, drawing it down and spreading the black leather open and off his shoulders. He kissed her as he let it drop to the floor, while she stroked her hands over his chest. She tugged at his shirt and he broke away from her mouth long enough to reach behind his head and pull off the fabric in one movement.

He laid her back on the bed and swiftly shed his own jeans before joining her, his cock now throbbing from being freed. She visibly swallowed at the sight of it. He spent long minutes playing with her nipples, teasing them with his tongue, sucking them into his mouth, and twirling them with his fingers. She clutched at his shoulders, moaning and writhing under him as he brought her higher.

"Please, Blue, More!"

He moved his head down her body, kissing the soft skin of her stomach, delving his tongue briefly into her belly button. She flinched and giggled, and he was pleased to find out she was ticklish before moving lower. Her legs parted without protest at his touch. He spread her wide and gently sucked her clit into his mouth, filling himself with the taste of her want. She cried out and pushed herself into him more, her hand threading through his hair as he licked and sucked at the pulsing bundle of nerves. He took his time, not rushing her to orgasm with a jackhammer tongue, but slowly stroking and savoring each taste and the breathy sounds she made. He pushed one finger into her weeping channel and she cried out again. He knew her body inside as well as out and hooked his finger deep to press against the spot that would drive her over the brink. He circled it, pushing his finger in and out of her and adding another, drawing the pleasure from her, long and slow. She clutched at his hair and writhed under his tongue, grinding and whimpering as he pushed her higher. He felt her losing control and reveled in it when she screamed his name as she came. He eased his fingers out of her and lifted up with one last lick.

He quickly ripped open a condom packet with his teeth and sheathed himself. He covered her body, holding himself over her with one arm and using the other hand to guide the head of his cock to her soaked opening. He pushed inside her slick channel, the feeling of her giving in and opening around him almost too much for him to handle. She was tight, clenching around him. Sweat broke on his brow as he worked himself in small movements, easing into her. She clutched his shoulders at his slow invasion, gasping as he delved deeper inside her with every gentle push. He finally sheathed himself all the way, nearly coming himself at the feel of her closing around him, pausing for a moment to allow her body to get used to his. He kissed her, giving her back her own taste, stroking his tongue in her mouth.

"You okay, baby?" he asked, grinding his hips into hers. She inhaled sharply at the sensation and her fingers dug into his shoulders. He grinned and repeated the movement.

"Oh! I'm—ah!—I'm good," she panted, lifting her hips to seek more of the same.

"Hang on to me tight as you can, darlin'."

He pulled back and drove back into her slickness, slow and steady, letting her feel every inch sliding in and out, drawing every last ounce of feeling he could. Her arms clung to his shoulders and she shifted her hips to meet every one of his deep slow thrusts and cried out when he hit the right spot. He held himself back, drawing out the time as long as he could, and when she climaxed again she came longer and deeper. The waves of her orgasm were more than he could take and he finally let go, yelling at his own peak.

Blue stayed inside her, feeling more than just satisfaction. This was where he fit. This was where he belonged. This was the other half of himself he had been missing. Wasn't it a bit ironic that the part of him he needed the most had been right across the street? It was a sobering thought that he could've easily let this moment pass by if it weren't for Psalm's persistent claim to be his friend. He finally withdrew from her, slipped into the bathroom to take care of the condom and rejoined her on the bed, lying close to her side, unwilling to have any space between them.

His head lowered and he kissed her trembling mouth. She was panting and shaking still from the intensity of their coupling. "Baby, you good?" He traced her lips with the tip of his tongue.

"I had a major crush on you in high school," she blurted out, unfiltered. "I used to dream of being here like this with you. It was more than I ever could've imagined."

The look he gave was warm as he ran a hand over her tangled hair. "I'm not done yet. You're not on birth control by chance, are you?"

She shook her head. "No. I haven't needed to be since Adam passed."

He kept touching her hair, pulling at the fine strands and arranging them randomly around her face. "You'll need to get on that soon. I don't want anything between us when I'm inside you."

"Um—does that mean this isn't for just one night?" she asked tentatively. Blue could see the vulnerability shining in her eyes and he had to tread carefully.

"I can't offer you more than this, Psalm. If you can see your way to have me in your bed, no conditions for now, I think we can do at least that. I want more. God Almighty knows I do, but right now this is all I have to give. Will that be enough for you?"

Psalm looked into his eyes and answered. "I won't lie to you, Blue. I want more and at some point, this won't be enough. But I told you once my door is always open to you. I meant it then and I mean it now."

Blue leaned down and kissed her softly, settling himself between her open thighs. A few minutes later, he reached for the next condom.

CHAPTER 17

Sam woke up with a start and was on his feet in a second, muscles tense, looking for the threat. He moved out of the warm dog house into the tall fenced run and sniffed deeply. The moon was covered by threatening clouds in the cold sky and he could see his breath in the winter air. Something was wrong. He looked back at the big house at the window where his little boy had been waving at him earlier. The window was dark. The hair stood up on the back of his spine and a snarl found its way through his chest and out of his mouth. Danger. He had to get out and find it. Now! He gathered his massive strength, his muscles bunched as he made a giant leap using the roof of the doghouse to power himself up on the fence. Catching the top of the chain link, he pulled himself over, coming down hard on the ground below. The shock in his joints when he landed was heavy, but he shook it off. Pain was something he knew and had dealt with much worse than this. He sniffed the frigid air a few more times and without looking back, he took off into the night.

CHAPTER 18

I floated in that place between waking and sleeping. Somehow I knew it was early morning, still dark outside, but right at sunrise when the world hovered on a new and glorious day. A warm male body was pressed against my side, holding me close with one arm across my bare stomach. I dream-smiled, knowing it was Blue in my bed. The words he said to me last night made no promises, but there was a possibility. I never thought I would have that again after Adam and certainly not with my first crush from way back in high school.

I stretched and shifted, feeling a bit sore in places I hadn't felt in a long time. It was a good kind of sore, one I didn't mind at all. I felt good. For the first time in months, I'd actually slept and slept soundly. Blue was awake as well and pulled the cover back, baring my breasts. I murmured a protest at the cool air. He covered one nipple with his mouth, teasing it into a hard peak while he brushed his hand over the other one. Twin sensations shot through me and I squirmed against him, coming awake fully with a gasp.

"Morning, baby," he mumbled, still sucking on my pink nipple. "Mm… I could get used to this."

"Oh, me too," I purred, arching my back, asking silently for more.

He gave it. Last night he played with me, igniting fires I had never experienced. I had a good life with Adam and a good sex life as well. At least, I thought I did. Adam was the only man I'd ever been with. I didn't count the one attempt I'd made after his death. Nothing Blue did to me was the same. He had no inhibitions and took what he wanted, drawing out my pleasure and his with a skill I didn't think was possible. He touched me in ways I only thought happened in romance novels and I surprised myself by not only allowing it, but luxuriating in it.

He switched his mouth from one breast to the other, sucking and licking. I moaned as he shifted over my body, settling between my spread thighs. I could feel his hardness pressing against me and I lifted my hips in invitation.

"I don't have any more condoms, baby," he muttered, letting my nipple go with a soft pop. "Tell you what, I'm going to go down on you first, then you suck me off, and we'll get in the shower together. Deal?"

He was already kissing his way down my body when his cell phone went off. The sound was shrill and almost as bad as getting doused with ice water. Blue groaned and buried his face in my belly.

"Fuck! I get so tired of that damn thing!" he groused. "Blake's on call this week, but half the time Molly ends up calling me anyways 'cause she can't find his ass."

He checked the number and his face changed from mildly irritated to major concern. He answered the phone and put it to his ear.

"What's happened?" he asked gravely.

I sat up, pulling the comforter up to cover myself. The tone of his voice had gone from playful to grim instantly. His face grew tight and I could see rage building in his brown eyes.

"I'll take care of it. You just get them to the hospital. Text me updates when you know something."

He hung up and was still. I could sense his iron control locking in and his eyes went dead. My heart jumped with a frightened apprehension. Not for me, but for whatever it was that he just found out.

He got up robotically and started dressing. "The kids were taken from the Lair last night. My mom and one of the club women were attacked outside and left on the deck unconscious. They were hit in the head with something and left in the cold all night. They're on the way to the hospital. I need to make some calls and get the boys up there for a search and put out an Amber alert and talk to the state police. Dad said there's security camera footage that shows Shorty Manacourt and Jonelle outside the Lair. Because of the emergency custody granted to me, this is considered kidnapping."

He was on autopilot, speaking his plans out loud, but I wasn't sure if that was for my benefit or his.

My heart dropped to my knees and I was split between

seething anger at Jonelle and panicky fear for the kids. "Oh, my God, Blue! What can I do to help?"

"I don't know. Might need you at the Lair. Might need you at the hospital. I'll text when I can. I gotta go."

He stomped to the bedroom door, paused, and rushed back. His mouth crashed down on mine and he kissed me furiously. Hard and short. He turned again and walked out, his phone plastered to his ear. A minute later, I heard the back door close. The silence he left was ominous, and the worry started. It was time for me to begin my day and get the soaping solutions started, but there was no way my mind could be on work today. Those two precious children were gone, maybe kidnapped by their mother in a petty attempt to hurt their father. What kind of person did that to their own kids? I got up, showered, and dressed quickly, not knowing what to do but needing to do something. My thought was to head up to the hospital and check on Betsey. The store would survive being closed for one day.

CHAPTER 19

Michelle crouched on the threadbare couch, still wearing her princess pajamas from the night before. Her hair was tangled and her teeth felt funny. Cody was tightly clinging to her side, still crying and whimpering. He was also still in his footie pajamas. His eyes were swelled up and there was a stream of snot that had dried under his nose. He kept wiping it off onto his sleeve since he didn't have any tissue or toilet paper and they were too scared to go find any. The whole place stunk of rot and looked like it smelled.

Jonelle and her friend Shorty had come to the Lair late last night and taken them out by flashlight through the outside, side yard, emergency stairs. Michelle had wanted to protest and to find her grandmother, but Jonelle was full of temper and had a short fuse. Cody was confused and sleepy. Michelle managed to keep him quiet and not stir up their mother any more than she already was. Shorty had hauled both of them up, one under each arm, and rushed them out of the building to Jonelle's waiting car.

Jonelle had driven a long time to this place deep in the woods. It was really dark and really scary when they arrived and even worse now that the sun had come up. Billy was there and was really mad at Jonelle. Michelle heard him call her mother a "stupid bitch" and "fucking cunt" over and over again. She only knew what "bitch" meant, but she knew the others were bad words too.

"Shells, I need to pee-pee really b-b-bad!" Cody lightly whispered. Michelle fidgeted on the nasty piece of furniture. She had to pee as well but didn't dare move. Billy was yelling at everything and everyone and had already screamed at Cody for crying. He had that glass thing in his hand and had been smoking through it off and on all day. It really smelled bad. Jonelle had smoked from the glass thing too, but not as much as Billy and Shorty.

"Da fuck were you thinkin', you dumb bitch!" Billy started again, pacing and sucking back more of the acidic smoke. "Fuckin' cunt! I done toldja we ain't takin' no kids! Too much fuckin' trouble. Fuckin' cryin' asses an' shit!"

Jonelle lay back on an old recliner that had also seen better days. "An' I done told you, as long as I have 'em, the state makes him pay child support an' I get a deposit in my account every month. Nothin' that asshole can do about it!"

Michelle knew they were talking about her and Cody and Daddy. She was out of tears at this point. She had stopped thinking about Jonelle as "mama" a long time ago and didn't understand why Jonelle hated her daddy so much, but she did.

"As soon as Shorty gets back with the money, we're

outta here. Them biker assholes almost got him yesterday. Stupid fucker! You want them kids? You keep 'em quiet and keep up, 'cause I ain't waitin' for no one!"

Michelle heard Cody whimper and move around. He was about to pee his pants and that would probably set both Billy and Jonelle off. So far, neither adult had hit them, but Michelle was afraid that could change anytime.

"Mama, can we go to the bathroom? We gotta pee real bad," she said in the smallest voice she could muster.

Jonelle rolled her eyes and flicked her hand down the short hallway. "Go do whatcha gotta do and then get back here."

The toilet was cracked and leaked, but at least it still worked. There wasn't any toilet paper, but there was a roll of paper towels. Michelle let Cody go first and then finished her own business. She took a few of the paper towels and wet them in the sink, trying to clean both her and Cody a bit.

"I w-w-wish we had s-s-some of Psalm's soap right now!" Cody wailed softly. "It smells really good."

"I know, Cody. I wish we did too."

Cody began to cry again, making her wonder how many more tears he had in him. "I want to go home. I want Daddy!" he sobbed.

Michelle didn't know which he really wanted, since home was different than where Daddy lived.

"Shells! Cody! Get your asses back in here!" They scurried at the sharp yell from their mom.

Billy was barking on his phone. Jonelle was watching him, a worried look on her face.

"What da fuck do ya mean you can't get to the money?" He paused.

Then he exploded.

"Them goddamn bikers ain't my fuckin' problem, shit for brains! You better figure it out, motherfucker! You get that fuckin' money and you get it the fuck here, now!"

He snapped the phone closed and threw it across the room. "Goddamn fuck!" he stomped around, holding his head. "Fix me up a goddamn rock, baby."

Jonelle sneered back. "You done had three already."

Billy's eyes bulged from his face and his lip curled back over his teeth. Michelle shrank back against the wall in fear.

"Fix. Me. Another. Fuckin'. ROCK!" Spit flew from his lips.

Jonelle paused for a moment, then rolled her eyes. "Shells, take your brother in the kitchen and get something to eat. Stay there until I call you."

Michelle took Cody's hand and led him into a kitchen with flowery orange and green wallpaper that was faded and peeling. There was an old Formica table with four chairs sporting cracked red vinyl seats and metal legs and old green refrigerator that rattled in one corner next to a matching oven with three of the four burner eyes gone.

The contents of the struggling fridge were much the same as they were at Jonelle's house. A half loaf of bread, peanut butter, a pack of bologna, and two cases of beer sat in the rattling machine. There were a few bottles of water in the door and a bottle of cheap ketchup that had fallen over sometime and had leaked into a gummy puddle on one of the shelves.

Michelle sighed and pulled out the bread and lunch meat.

"Can I have mayonnaise? I don't like ketchup on my bologna," Cody piped up, wiping his nose again on his sleeve.

"We don't have mayonnaise right now. You'll just have to eat it dry."

Michelle pulled two paper plates from a stack on the chipped Formica counter. She added a handful of stale chips from an open bag close by. Cody sat on the floor and wolfed down the food. She made her own sandwich and chips as well and sat next to him.

The kitchen was full of plastic Rubbermaid boxes and lidded, big buckets of stuff. The counter and sink were full of crusty stock pots and the whole place stank worse than the living room couch. Michelle didn't know what the setup meant, but in her gut, she knew it was bad. Her young brain was sending out warning signals like crazy, telling her she needed to get out and get out now. Something bad was going to happen and soon. She couldn't leave Cody. Billy already didn't like them, but especially didn't like the little boy, always calling him names and saying how he hated dealing with kids. She really didn't want to leave her mama with Billy, but what other choice was there? She knew Jonelle would leave them both in a heartbeat if it suited her needs.

Her eyes lifted to the back kitchen door. The dead bolt was way out of her reach, but it was unlocked. There was a pile of large towels in the corner stacked up that didn't look too dirty. She made up two more sandwiches of the old bread and baloney. There were no sandwich bags or wrap, but there was a pile of plastic grocery bags crammed into a corner. She wrapped the sandwiches in one bag and stuffed it into another, adding more chips and two of the water bottles.

"Stay here and keep quiet," she instructed her brother.

She left Cody on the floor and peeked around the corner into the living room. Billy was in the old recliner with his hand on her mother's head as it moved up and down between his legs. His eyes were closed and he was grunting and cursing with her every movement.

Michelle's eyes opened wide at the sight, but what really got her attention was the gun sitting on the table next to Billy's other hand.

She made up her mind.

Carefully, slowly, she snuck into the living room, crawling on all fours. The coffee table hid her for the most part and as long as she was really quiet she should be able to sneak all the way. She thought if her heart pounded any harder, they would hear it, but only sounds were the eager slurping noises coming from the two adults. She was terrified of being caught and tried not to think of what would happen should Billy open his eyes and see her not five feet away from his feet. She slid forward, trying not to make the floor creak. Picking up both her shoes and Cody's shoes, she backed out of the room the same way. Neither Jonelle nor Billy noticed.

Back in the kitchen Michelle let out a breath she hadn't realized she'd been holding. She was so scared, tears were forming in her eyes. She blinked them away. She had to be Daddy's strong brave girl now.

"Cody, we gotta leave," she said, putting the shoes on Cody's feet over the footie pajamas. "I got some food and some water. We can wrap up in a couple of those towels to keep warm."

"Where we going?" Cody complained.

"If we climb up the biggest hill we see, we can find Gramma's house. We'll go there." She slipped on her own shoes. Hers didn't light up when you stomped them like Cody's did, but they were still a pretty princess pink.

"I bet Gramma has mayonnaise." Cody rose eagerly from his spot.

"She does. She's got lots of stuff at her house."

Michelle stood up and grabbed some of the towels, throwing two around Cody's head and shoulders and doing the same for herself. The towels smelled sour and she wrinkled her nose, but there wasn't anything else she could see to get without trying to get past the two adults again.

"We hafta be real quiet now. Can't make any noise till we get in the woods and find a hill to climb. Got it?"

Cody nodded, a worried look on his face, but he trusted her.

Michelle nodded back and picked up the plastic bag of their meager supplies. She turned the knob slowly to the back door and tugged on it. A brief moment of panic had her stomach clenching when the door stuck. She tugged a bit harder and it reluctantly opened, screeching loudly in the process. Billy let out a huge bellow at the same time.

"Goddamn fuck!"

Michelle and Cody froze in terror, waiting for him or Jonelle to come barreling in the room. A minute or two later, when no one rushed into the kitchen, Michelle dared to move, pushing Cody through the door into the cold air. She followed with the bag and turned the knob to close the door without the latch clicking. The back of the house was full of overgrown grass. They moved through it as best as they could. When they reached the tree line, Michelle took one last look over her shoulder at the falling apart house. A single tear ran down her face. She turned and led Cody into the woods.

CHAPTER 20

Blue drove up to the house he and Jonelle once shared. He had spent the afternoon first at the Lair and then at the hospital. The security cameras at the Lair showed Jonelle and a local thug by the name of Shorty coming out of the Lair with Cody and Michelle. He and Brick watched as Shorty raised a baseball bat, swinging and connecting first with Donna's head and then with Betsey's. Both women were stable, but Betsey was still unconscious. Brain damage was a strong possibility, but the doctors would not be able to assess that until she woke up. Hopefully she would.

Brick went glacial with absolute rage when he saw his woman get hit. The fury pouring from him froze the very air around him and every club member burned with the icy cold of his wrath. His voice when he spoke to Blue was subzero.

"I got respect for you, son, and I got respect for the law. But I also got respect for justice and sometimes them things don't line up. You and I don't see eye to eye on that all the time, and I been easy about it for a long time, but I'm gonna tell you now, this is one time I'm gonna ask the law to stay outta my way."

Blue's jaw gritted. He knew this meant Shorty's days were numbered and maybe even Jonelle's. This was against everything he was supposed to stand for as an officer of the law, but as a man, a father, and a son, he was ready to put the badge in his pocket and join his club brethren. The fact that his children were missing and possibly in harm's way was enough to make him question the oath he took. In the club's history, more than one man had been "taken up the mountain" never to return. Blue knew this didn't happen often but when it did, there was good reason. His best bet was to find Shorty, Jonelle, and Billy before the Runners did. If he didn't, he knew there would be no trace and he'd have to make a decision that he would have to live with. He had given his dad a single jerky nod.

The house was a small ranch style, older, but still in a nice, safe neighborhood. Jonelle didn't like it and wanted one of the fancier homes in the new housing development, but this was what he could afford on his salary. He parked the car a few houses down. A club prospect was easily spotted, attempting to hide behind a row of hedges near the opposite side of the house. Blue sighed, thinking no one with any sense would approach the house with such an obvious guard dog. He waved at the man and entered the house he had once owned but hadn't set foot in during the past year.

The décor was the same, but the house itself was mess. Plates with dried-up food were stacked on the coffee table, papers and other bits were scattered around, and the trash bins were overflowing. Jonelle had never worked at a job, citing that she could stay at home to take care of the kids and the house while he earned the money. She had never been a great housekeeper, but this was worse than he had thought. He went into the kitchen and found a sink full of dirty dishes and more trash scattered on the counters and floor. The fridge held the bare minimum of food.

"Fuck!" The word burst from his lips as he slammed the fridge door. Anger and guilt raced through him at the way his kids had been living and how long he had allowed it to happen. He whipped out his phone and took pictures of the filth as he made his way through the house. It looked like both kids had been moved into one room, or maybe Cody had moved into the pink princess room to be near his sister. The sight of their clothes and toys piled neatly on one side of the room and the carefully made bed almost undid him, but he grabbed at his iron control and kept looking around.

He hit the jackpot in the main bedroom. There was a glass pipe and other paraphernalia sitting on the nightstand next to the bed he once shared with the woman he now hunted. It was out in the open, as if daring anyone to come and see what had been happening in this house. Blue snapped more pictures and slipped on some latex gloves. Under the bed, he found a duffle bag of money, the bills just randomly stuffed inside and several boxes of the crystal drug that had been floating around his town, killing people. Small plastic baggies and a digital scale completed the picture and there was no doubt he'd found the distribution source.

Blue raked his hand over his head and pressed his

forehead into the side of the sour-smelling mattress, his heart pounding and hurting. "Fuck!" he uttered again, but only the silent house answered him. Tears gathered in his eyes and he blinked them back. This was not the time to fall apart. He still had to find his kids and the people who had them.

The loud crash of a breaking window went through the house. Blue's head jerked up at the sound. He heard a man's voice curse and a thump as whoever it was made his way inside.

"Fucking damn bikers! Gotta fuck everything up. Stupid bastards!"

Blue slipped silently into the closet, leaving it open a crack, and drew his gun. His first impulse was to charge the man, but he needed to see who it was. His suspicions were rewarded in the next minute as Shorty ambled into the bedroom, squatted, and flipped up the wrinkled bedspread to get to the bags underneath. Shorty huffed and puffed, the sparse hair on his head greasy with sweat and his soft body stretched awkwardly. He grunted and groaned as he pulled out the money and the drugs.

"Fuckin' Billy! Thinks I'm his fuckin' servant. Like I got nuthin' better to do than run his goddamn errands. 'Shorty, get this!' 'Shorty, get that!' Fuck that noise. I'mma take this shit and gettin' the fuck outta— Oh fuck!"

His monologue stopped when Blue's gun pressed against his temple. Blue spoke in a voice colder than ice. "Where are my kids, you piece of shit?"

Shorty raised his hands, stayed sitting on the floor, and

assumed a placating demeanor. "Now, Deputy, I know you're not gonna use that gun on me, seein' as you're an officer of the law an' all. I was jus' followin' orders. Same as you do. I'm sorry, really I am,"

"I repeat, where are my kids?"

Shorty panted, his breath getting ragged and wheezy.

Footsteps clomped down the hallway and a moment later, the room was filled with several large bodies of some very pissed off bikers, guns drawn and pointed. Brick entered like the king he was, and the room froze to absolute zero.

Shorty cried out in fear and pissed himself at the sight of Brick's hard face. This was a man who completely rebuilt the Dragon Runners club with guts and a hard-line leadership. People were sometimes stunned that he held the power to decide other men's fates and could turn from being a lovable teddy bear into a fierce ruthless predator. He said in a tone that was calm and almost easy sounding, "Afternoon, Shorty. Now, you answer the good deputy's question an' tell me where my grandkids are at."

Shorty didn't hesitate. He whimpered, "I seen 'em up with Billy an' Jonelle at th' cabin." The blubbering man wiped his nose as it dripped. "They's fine when I left 'em. Billy wasn't gonna take 'em, but Jonelle wanted 'em real bad. We all are supposed to leave town once I get up there with th' money."

Brick poked at the duffle bag on the floor and several bags of crystal fell out. "This the stuff you been selling around my town? Selling to kids?" Brick inquired with icy candor. The other bikers shifted and Shorty tried to fold in on himself.

"What cabin?" Blue asked, his gun still trained on the piss-covered man.

"'S one off old Myers Road down toward the holler. Used to belong to Billy's uncle, back in the day." Shorty was openly crying now and could barely answer. "Brick, please lemme go! I didn't hurt them kids, I swear it! I'll leave town an' I won't never ever come back!"

Brick turned to Blue. "I'm thinking you need to be gettin' to the kids 'bout now. We can see to takin' care of Shorty here."

Blue hesitated, at war with himself over his job as a deputy and his life as a father.

Brick spoke softly. "You've been a Runner, Blue. You know how it is. Most time, the law and justice meet up just fine. Sometimes not. I think you know the difference."

Blue stood silently for a moment more and then slipped the safety back on his gun. "I'll call when I got the kids back." He nodded to the other Runners in the room and left. The last thing he heard as he walked down the hall was Brick.

"You got it right, Shorty, when you said you're leaving town an' ain't never coming back."

CHAPTER 21

I left the store closed for the day and went to the hospital to sit with Betsey. The woman looked every bit her age, lying in the white hospital bed with tubes in her nose, a large bandage around her head, and an IV in her arm. I had the thought that Betsey would be upset over the loss of her hair, since the doctor had shaved a big spot from the back of her head in order to stitch up the nasty wound. Being in the cold all night had caused mild hypothermia and she was also dehydrated. Donna wasn't in much better shape, but she had rallied faster than Betsey and was awake. Another sheriff's deputy had come by the hospital and questioned her gently, but she didn't have much to add. She hadn't seen the blow aimed at her head nor the attack on Betsey.

My hands were busy with a crochet hook and a skein of yarn, trying to make something resembling a scarf, but I couldn't find the right rhythm or pattern. Now the yarn was a hopeless tangle of red. I sighed for the hundredth time and starting detangling again. I knew this was a futile effort, but

I still needed to do something to keep my brain occupied. The kids were missing and I found out Sam was missing too. Dozens of different scenarios ran through my mind regarding all of them. I called Lindsey, the vet, to give her a head's up about Sam in case he turned up somewhere, but that was all I could do. My instinct was to run out and start looking, but where?

"Now what did that yarn ever do to you?" a raspy voice asked from the bed. Betsey had finally awakened. "Lord, have mercy! My head feels like a busted watermelon!" She grimaced and tried to raise her hand to the bandages. "This is the damn hospital. What the hell happened?"

Relief flooded through me and I hurried over to her side. "I'm so glad to see you're awake! We've been worried sick about you. I know your head is still hurting, but what about the rest of you?"

Betsey let out a lame *pshhht*. "I'll be fine once I get outta this bed and see what them lazy asses have done to my house. I hope they got sense enough to clean up after themselves. What time is it? Where's Brick 'n' Blue? They in court?"

I reached for the button to call the nurse. "No court today. I'm not sure where they are now, but both Blue and the club are looking into the attack and other stuff that happened last night."

Betsey shifted and groaned. "I was at the Lair, making Donna help me clean up after the party. Almost everyone had gone home and left me with the mess. I hate that! Brick, that sorry dawg, went up to bed, telling anyone who would listen he needs his beauty sleep. Hmph! He's just an old man trying to keep up with the young'uns. Shells and Cody were upstairs already in bed. Poor little lambs! They done been through enough lately. I gotta thank you and your folks again for helping them out when they needed it most."

She paused and lifted the hand not encumbered with an IV line to her face.

"Anyways, them trashcans we got up there were overfull and about to burst. I ain't gonna have trash like that inside the club 'cause you can get bugs real bad and I cain't stand no bugs in my house. Weren't no prospects or hangarounds to lug them things outside, so I made Donna help me. She tripped and dropped her side o' the can and bottles went everywhere, glass breaking and making a real mess. I sent her inside for a broom and dustpan and I was pickin' up the big pieces of glass when I heard something. I thought it was Donna coming back, but the last thing I remember is a pain in my head. Now I'm here in this hospital bed with my head still hurtin' and wantin' to know just what the hell is going on?"

I paused, not knowing if I should share everything, but this was Betsey and she wouldn't be satisfied unless she was in the loop. I took her free hand and held it while I brought her up to date.

"You were attacked last night and the kids were taken from the Lair. I think there's video from the security cameras about who did it. They are sure it was Jonelle and some other guy. I know there's roadblocks on the highways and both the sheriff's department and the Runners are out looking. Blue will call me when he has news."

Betsey's eyes, ringed in black bruises, started watering. "Oh Lord, oh Lord, my babies!"

Her sorrow lasted about a half minute. "I'm gonna catch that bitch and snatch her bald-headed a'fore I'm done! Call that damn doctor, would'ja? I need to get outta here."

She tried to rise but fell back breathing hard. "On second thought, can you call Tambre, Molly, Kat, and Eva? I need to get up to the Lair and have all my ladies round me 'bout now."

I smiled, thankful I wouldn't have to wrestle the stubborn woman to keep her in the bed. "They're in the cafeteria getting coffee. I'll text Eva and let her know you're awake, then give you some privacy."

Betsey squinted at me. "What'cha mean, privacy? When I said I need all my ladies 'round me, I meant *all* y'all. Privacy my ass! I'm sure it's hanging outta the back of this sheet they call a gown."

I laughed as I texted Eva. Yes, Betsey was back. I pressed the button to call the nurse as I texted Blue the good news about his mom, hoping to get a response. The phone buzzed back.

Blue: That's great, baby. I got a lead on the kids. Know more later.

Warmth filled my belly at him calling me baby. I felt secure that this was real and that we had changed sometime during the night into a couple. I didn't know how long it would last but I would take whatever I could get.

My thoughts were interrupted by Betsey's yell. "What in the fire did that doctor do to my hair?"

CHAPTER 22

"Come on, Cody, we hafta keep going." Michelle pushed at her younger brother as they climbed over another large rotting log. The woods were thick and smelled of earth as they trudged on, always heading uphill, and after crowning one rise, finding another.

"I'm so tired!" the little boy whined. "It's cold!"

"I know. I'm cold too, but we still gotta keep going," she repeated. The sandwiches and water had been consumed hours ago and both of them were thirsty and hungry again. Michelle pushed onward, determined that when they reached the top of the hills, she would be able to figure out where they were and what direction the Lair was. At least she hoped so.

Cody began to cry loudly and sat on the damp ground. Michelle wanted to yell at her brother, but she also wanted do the same thing he was doing. Her legs were tired and she was figuring out they were totally lost, maybe even walking in circles. As Cody continued to wail, she felt the tears gathering in her own eyes and running down her dirty face, but she had to be Daddy's big girl and take care of her younger brother. Her eyes lit up as she spotted some wild blackberry bushes. Most of the berries were gone, but maybe there were a few left.

"Look, Cody! Maybe we can find some berries like we do with Gramma." She pointed at the sparse bushes, hoping to get Cody to stop crying.

"Are those Gramma's bushes?" he asked, wiping his nose on his dirty sleeve.

"I don't think so, but we can go see."

The few berries that were left were overripe, but the children picked and ate them anyway. The juices stained their mouths and fingers. Cody laughed and pointed at Michelle's face.

"Your lips are all purple now!" he crowed.

"Your butt's purple!" she retorted, glad the crying had stopped at least for now.

The crackling of twigs had her looking up in fear. Bears were still out and about and her daddy had always warned of them. The sound of a familiar guff had her sighing in relief and she cried in earnest. Sam trotted up to the two children, his tongue lolling out and a big smile across his face as if he was just out for an afternoon stroll.

"Sam!" Cody cried out and threw his arms around the dog's massive neck. Michelle joined in hugging the animal from the other side. Sam sniffed and huffed in their faces, his tail wagging furiously.

"Where's Psalm?" Cody snuffled into the dog's short hair.

"I don't think she's here, just Sam." Michelle stroked over the canine head.

"Is he here to take us home?"

"I don't know, Cody. Maybe." Michelle was overwrought and happy to see the animal. Sam bathed her face with his tongue, cleaning off the sticky berry juice, and guffed a few more times. "We gotta get up and follow him 'cause he knows where home is."

Cody sighed but heaved his little body up and stood with one hand still on the dog's huge shoulder.

A rustling sound distracted Michelle and she looked with hope at the moving bushes. Maybe Psalm *was* around. Or Daddy had found them! Sam suddenly went stiff, his muscles locked in place like steel. The hair on his back rose straight up, his lips curled back showing his long sharp canine teeth as he stared at the bushes. His throat gurgled a low bone-chilling growl, but he didn't move from his place by the children.

A large black head appeared, pushing through the tangles. The bear was huge and lumbering as he was getting ready for hibernation. It spotted the children and the dog and seemed to be just as surprised as they were.

Michelle froze in fear; her brain scrambled to think of what daddy had said about bears in the woods. Cody screamed and grabbed for Michelle. The huge monster lifted up and bellowed at them.

***

Sam's reaction was instant the moment he heard and

smelled the other animal approach. The hair on his spine spiked up and his lips peeled back further, showing his strong massive jaw and long sharp teeth. He braced in attack mode, his super defined muscles swelling with tension as he changed into the fighting machine he had been trained to be. These were *his* children! *His* pack. How *dare* this creature threaten them! The bear sounded a challenge and Sam roared his anger. His voice drowned out the bear's in its demonic fury as he accepted. The bear charged and as it approached the trio, the fighting dog bunched his powerful body and leapt.

CHAPTER 23

Blue lay flat on the ground, binoculars in his hands, watching the dilapidated building that Shorty had called the cabin. It was more of an old farmhouse that had been let go to ruin. A chemical smell tinged the air and there was no doubt in Blue's mind he had finally found the source of the shit that had been floating around his town. There was also no doubt in his mind that both Jonelle and Billy were inside the house, as their vehicles were parked outside. He didn't see any sign of the kids, but that didn't mean they weren't in there.

Three other deputies were next to him, waiting for orders, and backup was coming from two bordering counties. Everyone was tense as the early evening temperature began to drop. There were many unknowns from the sketchy intel Shorty had given. No one knew what kind of firepower was in the house or what Billy's mood was at that time. Meth labs were also known to be unstable and there was no telling if this one was okay or about to blow sky high.

"I'm going in for a closer look," Blue whispered to his closest companion. "Keep alert."

He eased over the shallow embankment at the dirt driveway's edge and crawled painstakingly slowly to the house, keeping as quiet as he could. He pressed his body close to a partially open window, the stench of chemicals even stronger. He could hear shouting coming from inside and he softly clicked on his phone to record the words. Whatever went down, it would be a good idea to have something tangible.

"The fuck, bitch! Call 'im again!" Billy shouted.

"I done called him a dozen times already!" Jonelle shouted back. "He ain't picked up and he ain't gonna. That short shit's probably halfway across the state by now, running the Tail with all our money." She paused. "Betcha he took my kids!"

Something broke against the wall. "Fuck, woman! That dumbass ain't got your kids! Them little shits snuck off while you was sucking my cock! You saw! The goddamn door was open!"

Blue both felt relief and worry at the same time. The kids had escaped that cesspool, but were now wandering through what amounted to wilderness that was far from safe.

Jonelle turned on the waterworks. Blue had little sympathy, as he had witnessed her crocodile tears more than once. "That's my little girl and boy you're talkin' 'bout!" she whined, trying to sound pitiful.

Billy wasn't buying it either. "Shut the fuck up, bitch, and fix me another rock."

Her tears dried up instantly. "You done had four already!"

A loud slap of flesh on flesh and a thud sounded. Blue heard Jonelle cry out.

"You deaf, ya fuckin' bitch? I said fix me another fuckin' rock!"

Blue drew his gun and eased his head to the edge of the dirty window screen, taking care not to make any noise or be noticed. Billy was pacing back and forth, clearly agitated. He scratched at his arms and puffed hard at the cigarette in his mouth. Jonelle was on the floor, blood dripping from her split lip. She crawled to the rickety coffee table and started doing what Billy ordered. Several glass pipes and a small pile of crystals littered the table's top, along with a gun. That was the only weapon Blue saw and in Billy's frantic state anything could happen, but he would have to get to the gun first. Blue watched as Billy forcefully poked at his phone.

"Shorty, you motherfuckin' asshole! Get your fuckin' ass over here now! You take my money, I'mma fuckin' hunt you down and fuckin' gut you like a fuckin' fish!"

Blue's jaw clenched hard enough to crack his teeth as he watched Jonelle hand the twitchy man a glass pipe and a lighter. Billy flicked on the lighter and sucked hard at the pipe, filling his lungs and holding his breath before letting it out in a long puff of acrid smoke. He undid the top button of his oversized shorts and pulled out his penis. He grabbed Jonelle's hair and pushed his bony hips into her face.

"Make yourself useful while you're down there, bitch."

Jonelle meekly obeyed, opening her mouth and sucking

him in. He rammed into her throat, using her hair as leverage. He grunted as he thrust over and over again, not paying attention to the gagging sounds coming from the woman as she struggled to keep up with his demand.

Blue's gut churned as he watched his ex-wife's face get raped. His first instinct was to rush in and stop the abusive man, but the officer in him knew there was more at stake. He looked over to where the other officers were hidden and signaled for them to approach. Three more backup officers had shown up and all of them moved to surround the house, guns drawn and pointed.

Blue looked back into the window. Billy had finished and was sitting on the couch with another cigarette in his hand. Jonelle was up from the floor, wiping at her mouth and spitting red on the floor.

"Didja hafta be so goddamn rough?" she complained.

Billy just grinned and puffed at the white stick. "You love it, baby." He leaned his head back on the slouching couch cushions. "Now go fix me somethin' to eat."

Jonelle grumbled but moved to go into the kitchen. Billy closed his eyes and relaxed. Blue thought it was their best chance. He moved to the front door, careful not to make the warped planks creak with his weight. He gave a hand signal to the officers positioned on either side of the door. They nodded back in readiness. Blue raised his foot and kicked the door in, breaking the flimsy lock. The door popped inward with a loud bang.

"Police! Get your hands up!" he yelled, sprinting into the room and aiming his gun at the startled Billy.

"What the fuck?" the lounging man yelled, bolting upright. Jonelle screamed from the kitchen and came running back.

"Get down! On the ground!" Shouts from Blue and the other officers filled the room. "You're under arrest for—ah!" Blue started saying just before Jonelle cussed and threw a plate at his head. It was paper, so it didn't hurt, but the flying object distracted him long enough for Billy to snatch up the gun and start firing wildly at everyone. Blue felt a burn in his bicep as he dove for the crazy man. He ignored the pain as he drew back his fist and landed it square on Billy's nose. Blood spurted everywhere and the fight went out of him as he crumpled into a sniveling pile.

"You're under arrest for—for—fuck! For being an asshole!" Blue spat, as his fellow officers cuffed the snotty man. "Fuck!" Blue clutched as his bleeding arm. The bullet had only grazed him, but it was deep and hurt badly. "Anyone else get hit?"

"Just you, brother. Damn lucky that asshole has bad aim."

Jonelle wasn't through. Screaming like a banshee, she jumped on Blue's back, biting and scratching, trying to tear the short hair from his head.

"You goddamn motherfucker! You done ruint everythin'!"

"Ahh!" Blue cried out in pain, trying to shake off the violent woman without hurting her. He wanted to punch her lights out but managed to restrain himself while two other policemen pulled her off him. She was down on the ground in seconds, cuffed next to Billy. She spat in his direction, calling him names and cursing.

One officer looked at the mess of a woman and shook his head. "Can't believe you were ever with this one, Blue. She gotcha pretty bad."

Blood dripped from his temple and cheek where Jonelle's fingernails had scraped. Looked like he had new scars to add to the others.

"I'm okay. Call the rescue squad up here and call out the volunteer search group. My kids are lost in these woods somewhere and we gotta find 'em soon, before the sun goes down completely."

"Ten-four, boss man,"

Billy was cursing and blustering as he was half dragged, half pulled from the house by two deputies. Two others started bagging the evidence. Sirens were heard in the distance as more officers began to show up.

Blue watched as Jonelle was brought out of the house and put into a police car. She was still cussing and fighting, yelling about how she was going to sue for police brutality even though he was the one bleeding. No two ways about it. There was enough evidence in that house that both she and Billy were going to jail and going to be there for a long time. His heart dropped a bit thinking about how and what he would have to tell his kids. There wasn't an easy way and he hoped he could get through it. Custody was pretty much decided at this point, but he didn't feel good about the way it came about.

Blue stepped out in the yard amid the controlled chaos,

still holding his arm. He managed to pull out his phone and text Psalm.

Blue: Found the meth lab. Operation went sideways. Billy's under arrest. Kids are gone. They ran off earlier and are lost in the woods.

Psalm: OMG!! Poor kids! Are you okay? What do you need me to do?

Blue fingered the words in the text bubble. It figures her first words were concern for him and his children. He avoided telling her he'd been hurt. No use worrying her further.

Blue: Search and rescue teams need to be assembled. I don't know how long the kids have been gone but it's going to be dark soon.

Psalm: I'm so sorry! I'm with your mom and the other women still at the hospital and I'm sharing your news. Betsey is calling Brick and going to get the club members mobilized for the search. I'll call my dad and he'll get his church people started as well. Don't worry, we'll find them!

Blue clicked his phone off without answering. Psalm was the most optimistic person he knew, always trying to look on the bright side of things and never giving up hope. He prayed there was a happy ending to this story. There were so many bad situations that Michelle and Cody could encounter out there, his mind shut down trying not to list them. A paramedic came over to him and tried to get him to sit down so his arm could be treated. Blue resisted for a moment but then complied.

"It's pretty deep and needs stitchin' up." The paramedic spoke as he probed the wound. "We gonna have a fight about you goin' to the hospital?"

Blue hissed at the pain of the man's examination. "Probably. I ain't leaving here with my kids still out there."

The paramedic muttered "stubborn" under his breath as he bandaged Blue's arm tightly. "Just don't wait too long to go. You're gonna have a nasty enough scar as it is."

Blue couldn't care less about another scar. He had to stay on scene until the investigation wrapped up and then he was going into the woods, searching all night if he had to until his kids were back in his arms. Thank God for small-town folk who were gathering to help. Between the Dragon Runners, the sheriff's department, and Psalm's parents' church people, there would be several hundred bodies out looking for Michelle and Cody.

The sun was making its slow descent and dark was just a few hours away. Nights were bitter cold now and his kids were out there in the woods alone. Blue closed his eyes and prayed for a miracle.

CHAPTER 24

Marla Helton came out of her house wiping her hands on her apron. The sun was almost down, bathing the horizon in dark colors of purple, peach, and charcoal gray. The town had been buzzing all day from the story of the kidnapping and Betsey's attack. Psalm had called several hours ago to let them know of the lost children. Her church ladies had rallied the troops and the casserole brigade had started taking oblong glass dishes to the Rivers Edge bar for the club members to take up to the Lair. Betsey had been released from the hospital and was organizing food for the searchers now combing the woods for her grandchildren.

Marla shivered in the cold air. There was the smell of snow coming soon. Her husband Jedidiah knew these woods well and had joined in the search. She bowed her head again and said another prayer to the Almighty, asking for everyone's safety.

The sound of crunching twigs had her raising her head to the woods edge. Her heart leapt in her throat as she saw a blood-covered dog appear and two kids crowding next to him as they painfully made their way out of the wooded area just beyond the garden.

"Lord God Almighty Christ!" she declared, running toward them.

The dog was limping badly but kept steadily moving forward, the two kids huddling close and shivering. When he spotted the woman coming at them, he started whining and collapsed on his side.

"Ms. Helton! Sam's hurt!" Michelle cried out when the dog fell. Her face was covered in dirt and streaked with tears. The ragged nightgown she wore was torn beyond saving. Cody wasn't in much better shape as he squatted next to the heavily panting animal.

Marla dashed away the sudden moisture in her eyes and took control. She was a no-nonsense woman and knew how to handle most crisis situations. "Come on, little bit. Let's get to the house. We got a lotta phone calls to make." She bent over and scooped the dog up in her strong arms. Sam wasn't a lightweight by far, but Marla had been slinging hay bales and working a farm all her life. Carrying the animal wouldn't be easy, but she was determined. He didn't make a sound as he was lifted into the air. Instead, he rested his head on her shoulder as if to say "I made it. I'm done."

"Sam killed a bear," Cody said, walking next to the woman. His teeth chattered and he wrapped the dirty towel he was wearing tighter around his thin shoulders. His matter-of-fact attitude made Marla think he was in shock.

"He bit him in the neck and wouldn't let go," Michelle

said, her voice cracking. "Even after the bear hit him he wouldn't let go." She was wrapped in a nasty towel as well and just as much in a zombie state as her brother.

Marla clicked her tongue. "I'll call Doc Jackson first as that's the quickest one." She puffed as they reached the back porch. "I bet she'll make a house call for this here dog. Open the door for me, little bit. I'll call 911 and let your daddy know where you are. Might be we need a person doctor here too, and Doc Holbrook owes me a favor."

Marla managed to climb the steps with the heavy animal and placed him on the living room sofa. Blood still oozed from three parallel lines in the dog's side and there were more gouges on his back. One of his legs was badly mangled and looked like it could be broken. "Lord have mercy, Sam," she intoned as she picked up the phone and started dialing people. The kids crowded close to their canine savior, not wanting to leave his side.

"Is he gonna die?" asked Cody, his lower lip quivering as he ran his small fingers over the dog's thick head.

"I don't know, sugar pie," Marla answered. "Doc Jackson's on her way so we'll just have to wait and see. The Lord above takes care of those who do his work and I'm pretty certain that includes dogs. Sam's done been a guardian angel tonight and I know the good Father is watching over him." She pressed a clean towel to the dog's wounds. "Michelle, you put your hands right here and hold this. I'm gonna call Psalm and let her know you done turned up at the house. She'll take care of telling everyone at the Lair. Gotta call Agnes and get the phone tree started. You just stay right there and we'll get some food in ya while we wait for your daddy. I reckon he'll be along soon."

Marla went into the kitchen and said a quick prayer of healing for Sam and thanks for the children's return. She called Psalm and didn't preface the news, just blurted it out quickly. Then she started to bang around pots and pans. Best to stay busy, as people would be showing up soon and the kids needed feeding. She didn't pay attention to the tears traveling down her wrinkled cheek.

***

Cody and Michelle sat on the floor next to the couch, their hands on Sam's head. The dog's tail thumped sluggishly and Cody started crying. "Please don't die, Sam!" His little voice quavered. "I love you, please don't die!"

Michelle was shocked to feel the tears running down her own face. She hadn't thought she had any left. She buried her face into Sam's neck and sobbed, letting the emotions of the day take over. She was safe and could let go. "Thank you, Sam," she whispered.

Sam's tail gave one more thump and was still.

***

I swiped the screen on my phone to end the call and turned to Betsey, tears flowing freely down my face. I dialed Blue as I spoke. "The kids just showed up at my parents' place. They're tired and hungry but they're okay."

Betsey was sitting in the kitchen area, a bandana around her head covering the bandage and the small bare spot on her head. She clapped her hands and raised them high, "Praise Jesus!" she shouted, and began to cry. "Lord have mercy! My grandbabies are okay!"

Tambre stopped arranging the many casseroles that were scattered over the wide counters and went to hug the sobbing woman.

"Psalm, I'm really busy here. What is it?" Blue's words found my ear. My breath hitched as I told him the good news.

"Christ," he said softly, his voice breaking up as I listened to this strong, tough man lose it over the phone, crying in relief that his children were safe.

"There's more," I said, my throat still tight with worry. "Sam came with them. Mom said he was attacked by a bear while protecting the kids and is in pretty bad shape. He—he may not make it." I hiccupped, fresh tears welling up in my eyes as I thought about my beautiful, brave dog.

"I'm—I'm sorry, Psalm. I hope he does make it." Blue was trying to hold it together but the news of his children was more than he could take. He sounded distracted and I wasn't sure that my dog's fate really concerned him, but I had to forgive that as these were his children. "I have to go get to my kids."

I wiped a hand across my face and put on a smile in case someone was looking. "Yes, you do. Go now and I'll see you later."

"Uh-huh." He hung up. No endearments. No "I'll text later." Nothing.

When I heard the click, I felt my heart start cracking.

CHAPTER 25

The bell on the door jingled with a happiness that not many people were feeling. Both kids wanted to see Sam and Blue was relieved that the animal had pulled through. He was covered in stitches, wearing a giant plastic cone around his neck, and in rough shape but still breathing and still fighting. He whined and tried to get up from his bed on the floor of Psalm's shop when Blue brought the children over to visit. They both cried and curled up next to him, his tail thumping softly as he settled down with both his kids around him.

"I owe that dog my kids' lives," he told Psalm as he leaned on a display counter. The air was filled with spicy Christmas scents of cinnamon and pine. Psalm was slicing a loaf of fresh soap into bars. Somehow she'd made a bright green pattern into the design that resembled a decorated Christmas tree. Blue marveled at the woman's talent and creativity. He inhaled the piney scent.

"If you're still looking for a home for him, he has a place at my house. That is, when I get one. We're staying up at the Lair for now, but I know Mama won't mind having him there now. He could shit all over the floor and she'd still hug his neck and cook him steak every night for saving the kids."

Psalm smiled lightly and cut another slice; the wide, sharp blade thwacked as it went through the soft loaf. "Consider it done. I thought about adopting him permanently myself, but I expect the kids need him more than I do. I'll get the paperwork together this afternoon."

"Mmm" was his response. His life was still in an uproar. Complications with Jonelle, complications with housing, complications with the kids' schoolwork, and more, all piled on his back and he had to deal with it all at once.

He glanced over at his kids as they lay on the floor cooing and talking to Sam. The dog swiped his tongue over Cody's face, making the boy giggle and pet the massive head. Michelle was carefully stroking the animal's back as she snuggled as close as she could.

"We need to talk," he said, knowing those four words would put anyone on alert that the conversation was not going to be good. Her eyes darted up to meet his, and he saw a mix of caution, denial, and sadness in them. He had a feeling she knew what was coming, and a huge pain ran through his heart.

"I got a lot on my plate, Psalm. I need to get the house ready to sell, the one Jonelle and I had. Too many memories for the kids and for me. We need a fresh start since it's just going to be the three of us from now on." He noted the look on her face when he said "the three of us" but kept going.

"Something's not right with Michelle. She's too quiet. Doesn't say much at all and when she does, she's angry. She's been lashing out at Cody and at me, throwing and breaking things, just out of control. She has a lot of scars and I have to be there for my little girl."

"What can I do to help?" Her soft voice made his heart clench up. She was really more than he could ever hope for in a partner but he didn't dare take what she offered.

He lifted his eyes to hers, the pain in them obvious. "I can't see you anymore. I can't start anything with you or anyone else right now. It wouldn't be right or fair to dump all this on a good woman. You don't deserve it and I won't do it to you."

"Blue, I—"

"You don't need to be with a man who has this much baggage. It's gonna be a long time to get my life sorted and it may never get that way."

Her breath hitched. "Don't I get a say in this? I love you. I love your children. I know you're in a rough place right now and you have so much to handle, but I can help you through it. That's what partners do. Please don't shut me out. Not when you need me the most."

His heart caught at her words and he wanted to hear them again and again as much as he wanted to say them back to her. "Yeah, I need you, Psalm. I need you bad in so many ways, but my kids need me more. I let this happen to them when I should have been there. I should have been a better dad, should have protected them better, I—"

His voice broke and Psalm, like she always did, came to

him to put her arms around him. He buried his face into her sweet-smelling hair and allowed himself one last memory.

"I have to be a dad first and as long as they are suffering, you'll always be second to them. It's not fair to ask that and I just can't do that to you. I won't."

"I understand." She swallowed as she took in the firmness of his statement and he watched as she visibly reeled in her emotions. "I understand more than you think. I understand your grief even though mine was different. When Adam died, I thought my world died with him. There were so many what-ifs and regrets, but you know something? I learned that time does heal. Life moves on and with a little work, it gets better one day at a time. I still have the memory of Adam and it still hurts when I think about what could have been, but I healed and was able to reconcile building a life without him. I'm happy. You and the kids have to go through that process and it's going to be a rough one. I wish you'd let me help you with it, but I can't make you let me be a part of your life. I won't lie and tell you you're not hurting me. You are. Deeply. But I know something you don't. I will heal, and I will move on. I've done it before and I can do it again. Please remember I'm not going anywhere and my door is always open to you and to the kids, no matter what."

"You need to find someone else who can spend his life devoted to you." He meant to sound firm, but his voice lacked conviction. He took a step back and looked at her, hoping to find firmer ground.

She smiled at him with tears shimmering in her eyes. "That's the beauty of you breaking up with me, Blue. You can't tell me what to do."

He shifted his gaze to his children, still petting and talking to Sam. He couldn't bear to look her in the eye any longer. "Send me the paperwork for the dog when you can. I'll have Mama come by and get him when he's ready. Cody, Michelle, we have to go."

Cody's little face fell, but he got to his feet. With one last pat on Sam's head, he shuffled to the door. Michelle wasn't much better. She stood up and ran to Psalm, clinging to her like a vine. Psalm held the little girl.

"Come see me anytime, sweetheart. I've always got your favorite pink heart soap on hand."

Michelle gave Psalm a squeeze and then went to the door to wait with her brother. Blue was slower to follow. It was on the tip of his tongue to say the three words that would make him buckle, begging for her forgiveness. That this was one big mistake and that he wanted them to be together.

"Take care of yourself, Psalm."

With that statement, he and the kids left the store, Blue feeling more than ever like he'd left a piece of his soul behind.

***

I watched them leave and managed to hold myself together until I heard the engine fade away. I was glad the store was empty so I could let go. I cried. God, how I cried! Big loud wracking noises came out of me as I lost control. Waves of hurt ran through me, followed by rage. How dare he do this to me again? Lead me into thinking he cared about me and that we had a future. How could I let myself be taken in by him? Thinking that our time on the bluff was the beginning of something wonderful and having that yanked away? My mind spun through thought after thought, and emotion after emotion.

"He doesn't care about me," the voice in my head spat.

He does care, my heart insisted. *He thinks he's doing right by letting me go.*

"He's not right. He's wrong for treating me this way."

He has to take care of his kids.

"I can help those kids. I love them so much!"

He has so much bullshit to deal with now, there's no room.

"I don't take up much space."

He's still a good man.

"He's an asshole!"

No, he's still a good man. He's just blinded by life.

"He may never see again. He may stay miserable and blind the rest of his days."

We all have to take chances and make choices.

"What choices do I have?"

Listen to your own words. Time heals. I can choose to be happy. I've done this before. I can do it again.

Somehow I found myself on the floor next to Sam. He was whining and now bathing my face with his rough tongue. I laughed and petted his head, running my hand over the ridge between his eyes and feeling the hardness of the skull underneath. He sighed and yawned, giving me a bird's-eye view of his sharp teeth and the pink inside his mouth. He guffed at me, and the fresh odor of doggie breath wafted through the air.

"Oh Sam! You need some of those dental chews, pal."

I got up as my cell phone rang. It was Lindsey, calling to ask about Sam's condition and to ask if I was ready for another foster dog.

"This one is a Doberman someone found in the Walmart parking lot. Poor thing won't let anyone touch her without crying. She's underweight and has skin mites. This is a bad one. She's going to need some extra special attention and a lot of TLC. I know you've got a lot going on, but can you handle this? I don't know of anyone else who would be able to get through to her but you."

I wiped my tears and the doggie slobber from my face. Life has only one direction and that's forward. "Think she'll get along with the other dogs?"

"I'm honestly not sure, but she's so scared of her own shadow, she may do best with some other canine love. You okay? You sound funny."

I smiled at her concern. Blue may not be around anymore, but that didn't mean I was alone. "I've been better, but I'll be just fine."

CHAPTER 26

Blue threw another load of trash into the giant dumpster outside his house and wiped the sweat from his brow. Even in the bright sun and the cold winter day, he was sweating like crazy. The last few months had gone by in a blur and he'd barely acknowledged the holidays.

First, he'd had to tell the children their mother was going to prison for a long time. Their reaction was not what he expected. Cody cried very little and clung to him more for show, but Michelle's response concerned him more. She was quiet as she sat on his lap. Too quiet. No tears fell from her eyes and she didn't seem surprised by the events, shrugging them off like they were no big deal. There was damage there that he would have to deal with and he hoped he knew how. An emergency hearing was made concerning custody and the kids were permanently placed with him. He'd had to testify in court where Jonelle appeared in prison orange as her parents didn't have the means to post bond a second time. The charges were many and included manslaughter of the teenagers who had lost their lives to the drugs she and Billy had distributed. The sentencing trial was coming up and if convicted, both she and Billy would be put away for a long time. Even at the crisis hearing for custody, she'd stuck her nose in the air and cussed at him, the judge, the bailiff, and anyone else she laid eyes on in the courtroom.

Second, after the incident at the meth lab, it was discovered that the drug route was even deeper and longer than originally thought. There had been a whole network of cookers and dealers in other small cities scattered throughout the area, big enough to cross three state lines. The sheriff had found out the FBI had been working the drug case from the other end of the pipeline and had happily turned over all the collected evidence to them, making it their big bust instead of Blue's. Ultimately, Blue didn't mind as he had enough to handle without adding that bit of fame to his name. He had no interest in being interviewed on national television and was fine with just being the anonymous town deputy.

Even that fifteen minutes of fame would be too much for him to handle. His life was so up in the air with two kids full-time, house in shambles, life in chaos. He just didn't have any more to give.

Blue heaved another armful of debris into the dumpster and listened to the clang as it hit the sides. The noise nearly covered the growl of a motorcycle making its way down the long driveway. Blue looked up to see his father kick out the stand and lean his big cruising bike on it. It was winter and generally no one rode bikes during this part of the season, but Brick rode year-round, only stopping if there was ice on the roads. He took off his helmet and leather riding gloves, tucking them in his jacket pocket as the bike steamed gently in the cold air.

"Your mother wants to know how the work's going."

Blue grinned, knowing his dad wanted to know himself. "Going good. Got the bathroom and kitchen done. I owe the club a big thanks for pitching in on the painting and floor finishing. Realtor says he's gonna be taking pictures and listing it next week. Hope it sells quick. I know Mom's having the time of her life with the kids, but it's past time we moved out and on with our lives."

Brick grunted. "No debt for a brother. You know the club's gonna help out no matter what. Them's my grandbabies too, ya know." He stayed silent for a moment. "Jonelle sign them papers yet?"

Blue's face darkened a bit. "Yeah, no contest. Gave up her parental rights without a squeak of protest. I don't know if it's supposed to be a noble gesture or if she really doesn't give a shit. Either way, the kids have to deal with it and, God help me, I know it's for the best but it still ain't right."

"No, son, it ain't. Not too sure 'bout a woman ready to give up her young'uns like that, but on t'other hand, she wasn't too much of a mother in the first place. They got a lot of people around 'em who love 'em and will always be there for 'em. They had it bad when they were with their mother and as much as it sucks, sometimes a clean break is best. Y'all can get your lives back on track sooner 'stead of drawin' it out and makin' life worse in the long run. They're both in counseling and your mama says they're doing pretty good with everythin'."

It was Blue's turn to grunt. He pulled off his work gloves and tossed them onto the wooden porch.

"I'd offer you a beer, but there's no fridge in there anymore."

Brick stood back and looked at the front of the house. "Ain't bothered about no beer."

"Heard Table's coming back to town. Something going on I need to know about?"

Brick kept his eyes on the house. "Yeah, Table's coming back for a spell. Don't rightly know much about it, but he's a brother. If there's trouble, we'll handle it."

"Law trouble?"

"Could be anything, but you know Table. He wouldn't bring no trouble here 'less he had good reason. If we got the need, I'll be callin' you and if not, the club will handle it."

Blue knew arguing with his father was futile, and at that moment, there was nothing for him to know. He turned and looked at the structure in front of him.

The house was freshly painted and shone like it was the first day he bought it and moved his budding family into it. He thought there were some good memories somewhere, but he couldn't find them. All he could think about was the heartache and misery that had come from that house. He envisioned all the bad stuff being thrown away with every load he threw into the dumpster and with each contraction of his muscles, he felt lighter and lighter. He hoped his kids would be ready for the next move.

"So whatcha gonna do now, son?" Brick asked.

Good question, thought Blue.

"Can't do much until the house sells and I have some working capital. I'm almost flat-ass busted broke, but without having to pay Jonelle's bills, I can finally get a bit put back. Got a lock on a rent-to-own condo the kids and I can move into next month that's got three bedrooms. The place has a pool and a playground and is close enough to the school so they can stay in the same one."

"Rent-to-own, eh? Your mother wishes you'd let us help." This was Brick's way of saying *he* wished Blue would let them help.

Blue smiled at the older man in understanding. "I get it, Dad. You get that I need to do this myself, right? You and Mom already do enough for me and the kids."

"You know help is there if you need it. No markers." Brick pulled out a pack of cigarettes and began to light one. "Don't tell your mom. I don't sneak 'em often, but sometimes I get the hankerin'. I figure the good Lord let me live this long, he won't mind if I indulge a time or two."

Blue chuckled. "I won't tell if you won't," he said, holding his hand out for the pack. He pulled a slim white stick out and lit it.

"Good woman, your mama. Been with me through thick and thin. In all the years, all the club shit going on, she never once left me. Even when I sampled another woman a time or two on the road, she'd bitch me out, but she stayed with me. I was a lot younger and stupider then, and it took me a while to recognize what was in front of me. Never looked at another woman since. She's a great mother, great partner, best friend, best support I've ever had. Means more to me than life and the only woman I've ever wanted to put a ring on her finger. We been together over forty years and she still takes my breath away. I feel like the luckiest man in the world to have a good woman like your mom by my side, puttin' up with my shit and stickin' by me. Best wish I can ever have for you, son, is you find the same."

Blue stubbed out the half-smoked cigarette against the side of the dumpster and tossed the end inside. He knew where this was going. "Don't start, Dad. I got my reasons and two of them are sitting with Mom at the Lair. I got too much shit to deal with to drag a good woman down with me. Sometimes I feel buried in it so deep, I'll never get clean. I can't do that to her."

"Good woman ain't a burden. She ain't something you have to deal with, son. A good woman is an anchor. Not someone to hold you down, but someone to help keep you grounded and give you something to hold on to. You ain't got no anchor, Blue. The kids ain't got no anchor. Far as I can see, you got a good one right in front of you and you're too damn scared to take hold of it."

Blue was getting angry. "Leave it alone, Dad. She's better off without me."

"You so sure?" Brick fired back. "Maybe you're the anchor *she* needs. Didja think about that? Seems to me you're being a mite selfish."

Blue was incredulous. "Selfish? What the hell are you smoking?"

"Didja ever think that maybe she needs you just as much as you need her? Your mama is happiest when she's takin' care of people. You seen how she mamas on everyone at the club. Seems to me Ms. Psalm is the same kind o' woman. She loves them dogs o' hers like crazy an' I 'spect she loves them young'uns too. I bet there's room in that big heart of hers for one more."

Brick paused and stubbed out his half-smoked cigarette. "You got any a' them Altoid mints? Your mama will lose her shit 'n' have my hide if she smells smoke on me."

"In the truck." Blue gestured.

The older man pulled out the red-and-white tin and tossed four white mints in his mouth. He replaced the tin and moved to mount his bike, crunching as he went. "Just think on it, son. You got more to offer than you think you do. Might be you already got all that woman wants or needs from you. Be a shame to waste it."

Blue watched as the gently steaming bike made its way down the driveway to the main road and roared off. His jaw clenched, partially in anger at his father's meddling and partially in guilt at the wise man's words. He pulled on his work gloves and lifted another load of trash, wishing it was that easy to clean up his life.

Maybe it was.

He paused his work and looked at the house again. The foundation was strong and the bones of the house unbroken. He was still going to sell the house no matter what, but he knew that whoever bought it would have a solid place to build a family and a future. Did he have something solid with Psalm and threw it away?

Blue closed his eyes as the doubts, arguments, and feelings of guilt hit him yet again. He pulled out the small sliver of soap he kept in his pocket and passed it under his nose. It was too small to use in the shower anymore, but he couldn't bear to throw it away. He inhaled the scent deeply, feeling her presence. He had kept her number and her texts to read when he was in bed as he couldn't bring himself to delete them. He had been avoiding the coffee shop in the mornings but had made a point of discreetly checking out the store from a distance several times a week, just to get a glimpse of her during the holidays. He had torn his own heart out just as badly as he had torn hers and at the time he'd thought he was doing what was right, but if that was the case, why did it still hurt like hell?

"A good woman is an anchor. Not someone to hold you down, but someone to help keep you grounded and give you something to hold on to."

His dad's words haunted him as he tucked the last of the bar back in his pocket.

"Far as I can see, you got a good one right in front of you and you're too damn scared to take hold of it."

Blue sighed and dropped his head into his hands. "I fucked up again. I fucked up so bad this time, I can't fix it."

"I bet there's room in that big heart of hers for one more."

CHAPTER 27

I sat up in bed, waving my hand in front of my face trying to disperse the fragrance of doggie flatulence. My newest foster, Cuddles, was a Chihuahua and Dachsund mix, and I marveled that an odor that foul could come from a body so small. Miko and Prince, also new fosters, sniffed and shifted off the bed. Miko was the large female Doberman that had been found tied up and abandoned at the local Walmart. It had taken me weeks to earn her trust, but she got there and was now ready for a forever home. Prince was a ragtag Lhaso Apso mix with more hair than the other three combined. Dion was still with me after Sam had been adopted by Blue and his kids, but he was being considered by an older couple and would soon be leaving me.

"Oh, Cuddles! What did you eat?" I scolded as I climbed out of bed. She perked her ears up at my voice and gave me a proud doggie grin.

Out of habit, I looked across the street to the dark apartment. Someone else was renting it now and was a late sleeper. There was a light dusting of snow on the ground and more was coming. I needed to get my day started as I had a huge pile of boxes to ship and a butt ton of soap to make. The holidays were over and I'd spent the majority of the time working my store and filling Christmas orders. It seemed everyone and his brother wanted fancy homemade soap as gifts this year. Therefore, my bank account was full and my shelves were almost empty. Next up was Valentine's Day, and I was glad to be busy as it provided a great distraction to the ache in my heart I was learning to live with.

Blue had stopped coming to Mountain Perks for his morning coffee and I greatly missed that ritual. I knew he was working with his kids, trying to rebuild his relationship with them and heal his fractured family, but I hadn't expected him to cut me off so completely. I'd seen him around town in his capacity as a sheriff's deputy and even heard rumors he was getting ready to make a run for the sheriff's office at the next election. I wished him well. What else could I do?

The dogs zoomed around the courtyard, rolling and playing in the white stuff. I laughed at their antics before opening my work area and mixing the lye solutions for the day's production.

The streets were quiet as I drove the massive load of boxes to the shipping place. It wasn't open yet so I had time to get my coffee fix. The bell tinkled as I entered the warm, fragrant store.

"Hi, Pam," I called out, shaking snow from my mittens and pulling out my phone. "The weather app is showing a big one coming in tonight. I expect all the grocery stores are out of milk and bread already."

A large paper cup appeared in front of my face.

"Hazelnut latte with a shot of espresso and skim milk," a familiar deep voice rumbled, awakening those pesky butterflies I'd forgotten about.

My eyes shot up to meet Blue's and then dropped again. *Too soon, too soon,* I chanted in my head. *I'm not ready for this yet!*

"Hello, Deputy. You're looking well. How are Michelle and Cody? Sam settling in okay?" I was proud that I didn't crack and sounded steady and sure. At least, I hoped I did. It was hard to hear myself over the pounding of my heart.

"Michelle is getting back to her normal self. Cody is doing great as long as he has Sam with him. Those two are inseparable. I'm really busy, but I'm well. The holidays were rough, but we're getting our feet under us." He hesitated, then asked, "How are you, Psalm?"

He was still holding out the coffee cup and I reached up to take it. "I'm good. Christmas sales were way up this year." I stopped to sip at the hot drink.

"I lied."

The words had me coughing and choking. My face flushed from embarrassment as I gasped for breath. "What?" I managed to croak.

He let out a sigh and jammed his hands in his coat pockets before dropping his eyes.

"I lied, Psalm. I'm not well. Not well at all. Michelle is seeing a therapist, Cody won't let Sam out of his sight, I'm trying to sell my old house and praying I at least break even, I'm looking for a place to live for my kids, but that's turning out to be a tall order as I don't have all the money I need for deposits. The town is pushing me to run for sheriff and I don't know if I have the energy for it. The only positives in my life are that the drugs are gone from the town, at least for now, and if I haven't royally fucked up again, you."

I jumped at his words. "Me?"

He raised his eyes and met mine with an intense laser focus.

"I've been empty for a long time, Psalm. So fucking long, I didn't recognize what was right in front of me. You fill me up, baby, but I'm greedy. I want all you have to give. I'll take it and want more. I've tried to do the right thing and let you go. You don't deserve a man saddled with as much baggage as I have who will take and take and take from you, but these last few months have been miserable without you in my life. You have no idea how many times I've picked up my phone to call you just to hear your voice. How many times I've driven by your store at night just to see if you're sleeping or working. I wanted you to find someone else, but the thought of you with another man tears my guts out to the point I can't breathe. I know I've hurt you and pushed you away, but I've finally got my head outta my ass and I hope I haven't fucked this up so bad you'll be the one to turn away."

He took my free hand and raised his other to cup my cheek.

"I. *Need*. You. You make me be the man I want to be and I hope to the stars and back that you can find it in your heart to forgive me again. Please, baby, give me another chance. I swear on all that is holy in this world, you won't regret it."

I was shaking, barely able to hold on to the cooling cup.

"How do I know you're not going to push me away again, Blue? I can't keep playing this game with you. It hurts too much, and I don't deserve that from you or anyone else."

His thumb softly stroked the skin under my eye. "I still can't guarantee the future, babe, but I'll fight anything and everything to keep you in it. *I love you.* I'm sorry it took me so long to figure it out, but I really do. I love you, and Shells and Cody love you too. Please let me back in, Psalm, so I can prove it to you."

My breath hitched and my lips quivered. I could feel my eyes growing wet and the tears would soon spill down my face. I brushed at them and closed my eyes. "I can't let you back in, Blue."

I felt him jerk back as if I landed a blow. I opened my eyes to see his shock. "I can't let you back in, because in my heart, you're still there. You never left."

Blue made a choked sound in his throat before pulling me into his arms and wrapping me tight. His mouth found mine and he kissed me in desperation and relief. I dropped my coffee but I didn't care. A light smattering of applause and whoops came from the few other early morning patrons.

He ended the kiss but still held me close, not wanting to let go. "I know you got work at the store, but tonight, I want to take you up to the Lair for a bit. Have some time with the kids and Sam, meet the boys, that sort of thing. I'll bring you home as I don't know how ready the kids are for us to be there as a couple, otherwise I'd want you to spend the night in my bed. We'll have to ease them into it, but it will happen."

I was oblivious to anything but the man holding me and just nodded my agreement. My heart was full and ready to burst. I knew in reality there were still a lot of obstacles in our way but the way I felt at the moment, we could take any mountain as long as we did it together.

EPILOGUE

Four months later...

"Shells! Get the pink box outta the truck and upstairs to your room. Cody, leave Sam alone and get your clothes put away. We're burning daylight!" Blue bellowed from the street outside my house, directing what he had dubbed "the big moving day." It really wasn't that big as between him and the kids, they didn't have much more than their clothes and a few odds and ends. I already had enough furniture and furnished bedrooms. Blue and I agreed to let the kids choose their own colors and decorate their rooms as they wanted. This was my home, and now I wanted to make it theirs.

"I need help, Daddy!" Michelle yelled back, tugging at the plastic Rubbermaid tub that held her American Girl dolls and doll clothes. Blue appeared and picked up the giggling little girl, slung her over his shoulder, and hoisted the pink box on the other one. Michelle squealed with delight as they disappeared up the steps to where her room was located.

Betsey and my mother were upstairs helping to make up the beds, Brick and my father were putting together some Ikea shelves for the kids' rooms, and I was heading to the kitchen where a ginormous crockpot of chili simmered for everyone to enjoy at the end of this day.

Life moved faster than I expected it to with Blue. I'd been wary that he would change his mind again, but it didn't happen and he stayed true to his word. We were together every day, either with each other or with the kids. He stayed with me on nights when Michelle and Cody had sleepovers at the Lair with their grandmother. I had been toying with the idea of inviting the three of them to move in with me but wasn't sure how the children would feel about it. Michelle was the one to break the ice.

"Why do you have such a big house?"

"I bought this house because it was large enough for my store and my home."

"No one sleeps in all the other bedrooms, do they? Not even the dogs?"

"No, the dogs like to sleep in the bed with me, even though they take up most of the space."

"Maybe we can move here. That way the dogs can sleep with me and Cody and you can have more room."

"What about your father? Where would he sleep?"

She rolled her eyes at me and blew out a *psssshhht* in a perfect imitation of Betsey. "With you, of course!"

It was a child's logic, but it worked.

Later, after chili and home-baked cornbread, we settled into our new night routine of bath time, book time, and bedtime. I read to Cody while Blue read to Michelle. Both kids were out like lights before the last page was turned.

I closed the door softly but not before Sam jumped up on the bed and curled up next to the little boy. His damaged leg had healed, but was still stiff and probably would be for life. It didn't slow him down too much. I watched Miko sneak into the family room and curl up on the sofa with Prince. Cuddles had been adopted, but now I had a new addition, Freddie, a large black German poodle. I had a feeling this dog would be the one for Michelle. They had bonded quickly and the dog didn't seem to mind the painted colorful claws and frilly hair bows. Freddie pushed into Michelle's room and flumped on the very pink rug beside the little girl's equally pink bed. It wouldn't be long before he was up in the bed with her.

I met Blue in our room with the TV on and muted. He was already in the bed, lying on top of the covers, wearing a soft pair of lounge pants and nothing else. My mouth went dry at the sight of him.

"Hey, baby. Go do your thing and come back to me," he ordered in a light whisper.

"Bossy much?" I whispered back. He just grinned and settled himself deeper into the mattress.

I huffed a bit but wasn't really irritated. I was thrilled to have him and the kids under my roof.

I cleaned the day from my face and slathered on my wrinkle cream, then put on a mint-green nightie. Blue's eyes lit up when he saw me approach and he stretched out an arm in invitation. I relaxed next to him and put my head on his shoulder. He kissed the top of my head and continued to watch the silent game.

"The children seem to have already made themselves at home. I hope they really feel that way," I mentioned, watching the players move the basketball up and down the court.

"If they don't, they will soon. You've done a great job with them and for them, Psalm. They love you and it shows."

"I love them right back," I murmured. I could hear his slow, steady heartbeat under my ear and felt the warmth radiating from his body. I was being lulled off to sleep myself when Blue shifted and reached for something on his nightstand.

"I love you too, baby, and I know this is faster than expected, but if we're going to be a family, then we need to be a family." He held open his hand and in it sat a small black velvet box.

My breath caught at what he was asking.

"Will you marry all three of us?"

I opened the box and looked at the simple engagement ring. Just a single small diamond in a thin gold band, but to me it was the biggest, most beautiful ring I'd ever seen.

"Will you marry *me*?"

I pulled the ring from the box and held it in front of me. My eyes rose to his and I gasped out a yes. He smiled, took the ring from me, and slid it onto my finger. "Love you, Psalm," he whispered before he leaned in to kiss me.

At that moment, several bodies burst into the room and bounced on the bed.

"Yay! We're getting married!" Michelle crowed as she threw her arms around my neck. Cody wasn't really sure about what the big deal was, but his sister was excited so he would be too. Sam and Freddie jumped up on the bed and claimed spots at the foot. The kids finally snuggled into their father and me, demanding that *Frozen* be put on the TV and not the game. As the Disney movie cued up, Blue's eyes and mine met again. I could tell he was frustrated that his romantic plans had been thwarted by a cartoon ice princess, but I was okay. I had a bed full of people and dogs I loved. I had a lifetime of this ahead of me and I was ready to cherish every moment.

ACKNOWLEDGMENTS

Thank you for reading Blue and Psalm's story. I hope you enjoyed it. Blue, Psalm, and all the other Dragon Runners are fictional characters, but the dogs mentioned in the story were real. All of them were rescued from bad situations by either me or another person in my family. I tried to put their individual personalities into the story but did mix it up a bit. Toto was indeed a loving mutt of dubious parentage who loved nothing more than to bask in the sun and get petted. Sam was really a pit/boxer mix who was abandoned in a parking lot in a box and almost died before being found. Buddy, Maxx, Dion, and Zeke were rescued and lived long comfortable lives with my brother and sister-in-law. Prince, Miko, Cuddles, and Freddie were the rescues I grew up with and who taught me to love having a dog in the house. It's painful to think that dog fighting rings still exist but thanks to groups like the Merit Pit Bull Foundation, dogs that are rescued can get rehabilitated and a fresh start to a much better life. I hope if you consider owning a dog, you'll think about getting a rescue animal. They really do win the doggie lottery when they go to a good home.

As always, I have to thank the people at Hot Tree

Publishing (Becky Johnson and her posse) for making this book possible. Without their support, I don't think I would have had a chance to come this far in publishing this book series and I'm forever grateful that you took a chance on me. A big thanks to Carrie, Liv, Brittany, Robert, Andrea, and Franci for their feedback. Kim Deister, thank you for your editing and fine-tuning. I'm learning so much! Y'all are wonderful!

ABOUT THE PUBLISHER

Hot Tree Publishing opened its doors in 2015 with an aspiration to bring quality fiction to the world of readers. With the initial focus on romance and a wide spread of romance subgenres, we envision opening up to alternative genres in the near future.

Firmly seated in the industry as a leading editing provider to independent authors and small publishing houses, Hot Tree Publishing is the sister company to Hot Tree Editing, founded in 2012. Having established in-house editing and promotions, plus having a well-respected market presence, Hot Tree Publishing endeavors to be a leader in bringing quality stories to the world of readers.

Interested in discovering more amazing reads brought to you by Hot Tree Publishing? Head over to the website for information:

WWW.HOTTREEPUBLISHING.COM